Praise for *Journey to the Parallels*

"In *Journey to the Parallels*, Marcie Roman pairs a fantasy world, in which people can step through porous boundaries into other dimensions, with a solidly grounded and deeply affecting portrait of a close, but unusual family. Amber, the twelve-year-old at the center of the novel, loves her quirky, single mother but wishes she were more "normal." Within this framework, Roman beautifully illustrates universal psychological challenges of growing up and coming to terms with one's family."

—Jan English Leary, author of *Skating on the Vertical* and *Thicker Than Blood*

"*Journey to the Parallels* is a must-read for tweens and readers of any age who have ever wondered what it might be like if we could step through the looking glass and find ourselves on the other side. A clever and thought-provoking read in the vein of Madeleine L'Engle and Margaret Atwood, this timely novel follows twelve-year-old Amber on her mission to save her family and return their lives to normal. But is normal really as good as she thought it was? From beginning to end, Marcie Roman's fantasy tale keeps us guessing while pushing her characters and readers to challenge what we believe about freedom, family, and, most importantly, ourselves."

—Suzanne Barefoot, editor and former middle school English teacher

"What happens when we actually get what we wish for? Twelve-year-old Amber sometimes longs for a more traditional family life, but when she gains access to a parallel universe in which society dictates exactly how families should look and operate, Amber realizes what a slippery slope defining "normal" can be. Author Marcie Roman creates a fascinating, repressive parallel world in which surveillance is commonplace and behavior is narrowly prescribed, even as she asks the question: is our own society really so different? *Journey to the Parallels* is hard to put down, its worldbuilding grounded by the perspective of a gutsy and relatable young heroine."

—Janice Deal, author of *The Decline of Pigeons* and *The Sound of Rabbits* (forthcoming)

JOURNEY TO THE PARALLELS

Marcie Roman

Fitzroy Books

Published by Fitzroy Books
An imprint of
Regal House Publishing, LLC
Raleigh, NC 27605

https://fitzroybooks.com

Printed in the United States of America

ISBN -13 (paperback): 9781646032181
ISBN -13 (epub): 9781646032198
Library of Congress Control Number: 2021943789

Interior layout by Lafayette & Greene
Cover design © by C. B. Royal

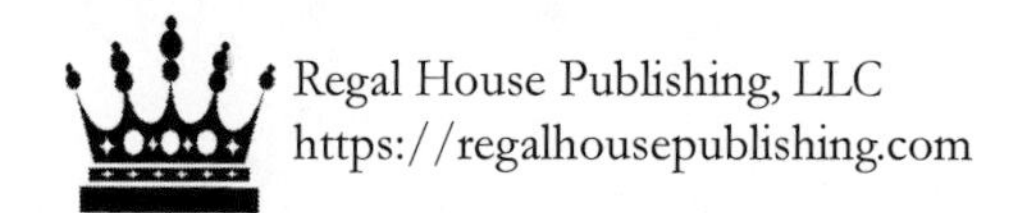

Regal House Publishing, LLC
https://regalhousepublishing.com

Printed in the United States of America

To my children, for believing

Part One: Here

1

On a sunny Wednesday morning in March, sometime between 8:15 and 8:30 a.m., Amber and Beetle's mother went missing. Wait, you might ask, how is that possible? Hadn't she been driving the car right up until they stopped in front of The Hastings School and she wished them a "marvelous day"?

That was one of the clues.

Amber and Beetle's mother *never* used the word "marvelous." Before that morning she had also never driven the speed limit, turned off the radio because it was a distraction, or, at a red light, sighed at her reflection in the rearview mirror and asked Amber, "Do you possibly have a comb in your bag?"

Amber did indeed carry a comb to use after PE, but in all of Amber's twelve years she had never seen her mother brush, comb, or otherwise attempt to tame the overgrown wilderness that her mother laughingly called "the Nest." When Amber was little, she'd half-expected a mouse or perhaps a small lizard to emerge from her mother's unruly curls. Amber couldn't imagine her comb surviving that battle. She shook her head and watched out the window as the car crept into the school parking lot at a painfully normal speed.

"Ta-ta," Amber's mother called as Amber and Beetle raced from the car.

Ta-ta?

⁂

Inside the school, Beetle headed down the hall toward his classroom while Amber took the stairs to the middle-school floor. The soles of her tennis shoes seemed to pound out *San-dra, San-dra, San-dra,* like the refrain from a song.

Amber had been addressing her mother by her first name since last year, especially when her mother acted embarrassing, which was often. Amber's mother had encouraged this response as a sign of Amber's growing independence. "I can think of worse nicknames. At least you're not calling me Sandy. *Blech.*" They were, after all, a family of multiple names. Beetle's nickname had come about when Sandra, destroying clichés as was her tendency, declared him to be as quiet as a beetle. (The proper term, of course, is quiet as a mouse.) His real name was Bernard, named after a great-grandfather. Or maybe an uncle. Like clichés, Sandra never kept her stories straight. As would be true for most nine-year-olds, Beetle preferred the nickname. He served it well since he also liked to scuttle into small spaces—under beds, in the back of closets, or, when there wasn't a space to hide in, inside his clothing. The necks of his T-shirts hung loosely from all his ducking in and out of them.

Amber was also a nickname, but not in the same way. Her real name was Ember (not named after anyone as far as she knew). When Sandra gave the name to the nurse at the hospital, the nurse assumed she'd meant Amber, so that was what was listed on the birth certificate. Whenever her mother called her Ember, Amber pretended not to hear.

Amber made it into class just as the bell rang, and by midday her mother's odd behavior had been drowned out by a surge of more pressing matters. She bombed her math exam (not a surprise, math was her least favorite subject), forgot her book for English, and still couldn't figure out what was going on with her friends, Debbie and Clara.

Amber had been going to school with Debbie and Clara since first grade, but they'd pretty much ignored her until last spring. That's when they joined the softball team, and Coach Dee asked Amber if she could "give tips to the newbies."

Amber didn't like to brag, but she was considered the best first baseman in the school, and that included the softball *and* baseball teams. Even Coach said so. Being left-handed helped (not so when it came to her handwriting). She was fast too, could outrun almost any ball when stealing a base, and had made the winning double play in last year's pre-season tournament. "You're the coolest," Debbie and Clara had raved when Amber came off the field.

Amber assumed they hadn't been friendly to her before because they'd never gotten a chance to know her—they were part of the rich crowd, while Amber and Beetle, who attended The Hastings School on full scholarships, were not. But she also knew that Debbie and Clara liked winning. Soon they were inviting her over after school to play catch and for sleepovers after the weekend games. And although they often teased Amber about her clothes and living on the other side of town ("I'd be scared to sleep at night," Debbie said), their own softball skills had bloomed with the friendship.

But with this year's season just a few weeks away, perhaps Debbie and Clara had decided their lessons were complete. On Friday, Clara had canceled plans for a sleepover—"Sorry, something came up." And yesterday, when Amber approached them in the hall, she'd heard a loud whisper of "Amber Alert" and saw them exchange a look. She'd tagged along as they walked to class and tried not to worry when she saw Debbie pass Clara a note.

Today, arriving in the lunchroom, Amber discovered they hadn't saved her a seat at the table. Amber was late to lunch because someone had swaddled her locker lock with neon-green duct tape. She didn't think it was meant to be decorative.

Seated in Amber's usual spot was Leanne Puttermer. (Leanne Puttermer!) Amber took the vacant chair at the end. No one spoke to her.

Don't, she ordered herself as her eyes started to tear. It wasn't like she had anywhere else to sit. She'd mostly been friends with the boys before last year, but there was no way she'd go and sit at one of their tables. Instead, she focused on her lunch box. Her mother had gotten it at a secondhand shop on Main Street. The lunch box was vintage 1980s, bright-yellow plastic with a picture of the Bionic Woman, just like one her mother said she'd had as a child. Debbie thought it was "super cool," and then showed up a week later with a red one with Wonder Woman on it, purchased new online.

Amber's mother had packed her a cheese sandwich, an apple, and carrot sticks. This had been Amber's lunch every day for as long as she could remember. Beetle was given the same thing, except his sandwich had mustard instead of mayonnaise and sometimes their mother mixed the sandwiches up and Amber had to suffer through mustard and Beetle's sandwich would come home uneaten. When Amber complained about the lack of variety, her mother shrugged. "Feel free to take over." Amber had made a shopping list that included tortillas, hummus, crackers, almond butter (the school was peanut free), oranges (the baby kind), and grapes. She knew better than to list anything fun like cookies—her mother rarely allowed sugary foods—or luncheon meat—they were vegetarian—but her mother had yet to buy any of the items. She'd probably lost the list. Classic Sandra. So another cheese sandwich it was, although Amber could tell that today it would be hard to swallow.

Tucked under the sandwich bag, Amber spotted a folded slip of paper. Amber was sure she was the only seventh grader at school, if not in the *entire* country, who still got motherly lunch notes. Not the *Don't throw away your retainer* type, or *Good luck on the test*, but random notes on scraps of loose-leaf paper, signed *xo Mom* ☺. Sometimes her mother would jot a poem, riddle, or joke. Last week it was *What did one eye say to the other eye? Something between us smells.*

Today's note read, *The witch warns of strange weather. Hope your mother has an umbrella.*

That didn't seem to fall into any of the usual categories, and it gave Amber something to concentrate on instead of the giggling from the other end of the table. The witch was a never-seen but often-referenced visitor to Amber's apartment. The culprit, according to Amber's mother, whenever items went missing. And items were *always* going missing: school forms, keys, winter gloves, sunglasses, and, most recently, Amber's favorite crop shirt with the sparkly heart that she'd gotten as a hand-me-down from Clara. Amber and Beetle would hear their mother yell, "Looks like the witch got us again." Until a day or a week or a month later when the item would reappear, often in plain sight, and their mother would yell, "It's about time, Witch!"

Amber had, for a long time, believed in the mischievous witch. Now that she was old enough to know better, the witch's thievery seemed to be one of the many examples of Sandra dodging blame. But Amber had never known her mother to put the witch's name in writing. Somehow it made the witch seem less made up and more like a real participant in their lives, like an out-of-state grandmother or a celebrity in the news. Also, there'd been nothing strange about the weather. It had been a perfect early spring morning. Sunny, edging toward sixty degrees. There would be no need for an umbrella. But the note was forgotten as Amber felt water soak her jeans. She jumped up and saw the tipped-over water bottle emptying its contents in her direction.

"We're sorry," the other girls chorused in a way that made it obvious that they absolutely, most certainly, were not.

&

After school, Amber and Beetle dawdled as they always did—sifting through their lockers, pretending they'd forgotten a needed book so they could double back. Their mother was *always* late and Amber hated to wait in the thinning car-pool line, like a kid not picked for a team (a feeling Beetle was familiar with, although Amber only understood it in simile-form). Just as the teachers started gathering stragglers to bring to the much-dreaded (boring!) aftercare program, Sandra would careen into the lot, spouting apologies about yet another job interview or her efforts to register voters for some local election that Amber was sure nobody cared about.

But today, as they exited the school doors, Amber saw in the front of the line the familiar station wagon with its dent-ed fender and streaks of dirt. (Sandra considered rainstorms to be the most efficient form of car wash, and March had been dry.)

Teachers walked through the waiting students calling, "Amber, Bernard!"

Sandra stood next to the car on the driver's side, even though the rule was to never exit the car while in line. Amber almost didn't recognize her because she'd tucked her hair into, of all things, a baseball cap. But their car couldn't be as easily disguised. Amber imagined it was as embarrassed as she was to have all those fancy SUVs and luxury vehicles staring at its rusted rear end.

"There they are!" Sandra called.

Amber saw Debbie whisper into Leanne's ear. Leanne looked in Amber's direction and snickered. Amber felt like sinking into the pavement, but she pulled Beetle along, climbed into the car, and slammed the door.

"Why are you here so early?" Amber demanded, fighting back tears. She would not cry. Not until she was home, door closed, her face stuffed into a pillow.

"Early? School has been out for ten minutes. I'd like to know what took you so long?"

Amber glared at her mother, then faced the window. From the back Beetle let out the squeak he made when he got in trouble. Just last week, he'd gone missing on the school playground and the squeak was how they'd located him, wedged between a wall and a plastic playhouse, stuck but unharmed. When Sandra was notified, she'd laughed and teased him that he should have been born with whiskers to help with his judgment.

Their mother kept to the speed limit, as she had that morning, and asked chipper questions about their school day. Amber scowled, and Beetle's responses were, "Okay. Yes. No. No. Okay." He tended to dole out his words with care, as if they were gold coins or Halloween candy (the only time candy was allowed, although trick-or-treating in their apartment building produced skimpy results). The radio was turned on this time, but instead of the oldies-but-goodies station their mother listened to, she had it tuned to a talk-radio channel. A newscaster spouted opinions about the last election.

Amber's mother *never* listened to political talk shows. "They've turned a democratic process into a sporting event," she'd said so often that Amber felt the message had been branded onto her brain, which, she imagined, was her mother's plan. Sandra preferred to read her news, and she insisted that Amber and Beetle also read up on the different candidates to "stay informed."

"My job is to raise Engaged Citizens," Sandra would say, as though it were a title worthy of capitalization.

Last fall she'd made them research the candidates for state governor. Amber had scanned the candidates' websites enough to answer Sandra's questions—and, it turned out, to get an A on a pop quiz in social studies—but then promptly forgot everything.

As the car crept along, Amber tried to tune out the newscaster—a challenge, since he seemed to have only one volume of speech. There were more important things she needed to think about—her math grade, her friends. She'd avoided them after lunch, but that wasn't hard since they'd avoided her too. Amber spotted her mother's baseball cap out of the corner of her eye and it startled her all over again. But what happened next convinced Amber that even though the woman in the driver's seat talked like Sandra and looked like Sandra—except for that ridiculous hat—the person in the car with them absolutely, unquestionably, was not their real mother.

2

For eight years Amber's mother had driven the same route between home and The Hastings School—right on Asbury, right on Church, left on Ridge—and for as much of those eight years as Amber could remember, Sandra had never once passed by the old brick building by the train tracks without announcing, "Wave hello to the Parallels."

The crumbling, single-story building was the last of its kind in an area that had turned over to office buildings and condos. It stood next to a small weedy plot that was littered with bottles and other garbage. On the south wall, faded paint identified the building as the School Towel Service. The front of the building was taken up by a reflective glass window. Each day on the way to school they could watch an image of their car, with their heads bobbing in the windows, pass from one end to the next, and then, coming home, enter and leave from the other direction.

"That's us but in a parallel universe," Sandra had explained to Amber early on, and then later, to Beetle, in case he'd been too young to understand at first. "It's like ours but with just a few details off." She'd used the same conversational tone she might employ when telling them about how their neighbor Ms. Pasquesi's missing cat returned home.

Amber had never been able to see through the School Towel Service window (due to its being opaque, as she'd learned in science), but she imagined what it might be like inside: mounds of wet towels transformed into fluffy white towers, steam and soap bubbles, and the sounds of swishing and spinning. In all these years, she had never seen anyone going in or out the front door.

Every morning they went by the building headed north,

and every afternoon they went by it headed south, and each time, *without fail*, Sandra would say, "Hello, Parallels." And, "Wish them a good day." And, "Tell them they should visit us soon." As if these proclamations were payment to a verbal tollbooth.

And for all these many commutes, day after day, year after year, Amber and Beetle waved. They greeted. They watched their reflections wave back. For Amber, the action had become muscle memory, like how to throw a ball to second, or count backward from ten.

When Amber was younger, her mother's insistence that these were actual living beings made her watch closely. Was it possible the reflection wasn't waving back at the same speed? Didn't it look like the Beetle in the window was wearing a blue hat instead of a green one? Now that Amber was twelve, she understood it was only the power of suggestion. Just another one of her mother's fantastical observations. If asked to prove it, Sandra would respond, "Give me a reason an old towel factory can't offer a window into a parallel universe." Or, in yet another mangled cliché, "Believing is seeing." Ghosts, witches, magic spells. Why not? In fact, the only thing Sandra didn't seem to believe in was organized religion, since she thought it limited the imagination. "Our religion," she had told them over the years, "is to keep an open mind." And boy, did their mother have one. And it wasn't just the Parallels. Entering the car with Sandra was like boarding an amusement park tour into the land of wacky make-believe:

The old stone house with the ivy-covered turret was where the witch, when not hiding objects, lived.

Those bushes in the sloping garden sparkled with dew because the fairies had been out to decorate. Thank them, but be careful what you wish for. They're tricksters.

See that old lady gardening in the straw hat with fake daisies? She's actually a fairy godmother taking a break from her day job.

And then there was Mr. Zagoom, the gray-haired "wizard" who drove a colorful spray-painted van with tinted windows that would sometimes speed by them in the other direction. Mr. Zagoom, their mother claimed, was also from a parallel land, and skipped between worlds to make up time on his way to work.

Beetle still went along with all of it. But within the past year, Amber had perfected the art of eye rolling and countered these claims with, as she saw it, a more rational explanation.

The witch's house was just some run-down place that the owners couldn't afford to maintain.

Dew was caused by condensation. She'd learned *that* in fifth grade.

The godmother was one of the many eccentrics who lived in their community, often seen grocery shopping in formal gloves or wearing flip-flops in the middle of winter.

And Mr. Zagoom? Well, perhaps he really was running late, but only in this world, and, like Amber's mother, believed the speed limit was merely a suggestion.

As far as Amber was concerned, on any other day Sandra had fit in among this crowd, with her graying hair and messy style of dressing in loose button-downs and baggy jeans, sometimes wearing the same outfit two days in a row. ("Don't judge a book by its look." Another misquote.) She was a terrible cook, rarely cleaned, never put away laundry, and took low-level jobs that she never kept for long, even though she had a college degree.

"Your mom's kind of unusual, huh?" Clara had said after Amber's mother showed up for a school play in a men's suit jacket and tie, and Amber just shrugged and smiled as if to say, *What can I do?* After the show, as the other parents clapped politely, Amber's mother cheered like she was at a rock concert. Amber was mortified. She hadn't even had a speaking part!

Clara and Debbie had perfectly normal mothers with normal jobs like real estate agent and personal shopper. Mothers who went to the gym and got their hair colored and brought their daughters along for mani-pedis. (Sandra's nails were so awful they shouldn't be described without a warning label.) These mothers let their daughters have cell phones and signed them up for fun dance classes. "Hip hop?" Sandra scoffed when Amber asked if she could take a class. "If you want to dance, put on music. Move to your own steps, not someone else's." She refused Amber's pleas that having a cell phone was a requirement to being socially active.

"I have my reasons," was all she said, and Amber was sure those reasons had to do with some ridiculous theory that a phone would drain Amber of imagination. Although Amber also knew that phones were expensive. Her mother was always complaining about her own cell bill, and she just had an old-style flip phone.

Perhaps it wouldn't have been such a big deal if there'd been another grown-up to combat their mother's strangeness, but Amber and Beetle didn't have a father. (Well, they did in the biological sense, but not in their day-to-day-lives sense.) Lots of kids at school had different arrangements of parents. Some, like Stuart Matthews, had two moms; or the twins, Miriam and Emily, had two dads; a few had divorced parents who co-parented; and some had lost a parent to illness. But Amber and Beetle were the only ones they knew of who didn't remember having any kind of second parent. Their father had disappeared when Amber was three and Beetle just born. Amber's only recollection was a faint image of a beard and long limbs. She couldn't be sure she hadn't mixed him up with a picture of Paul Bunyan in a book she used to look at back then.

As Amber got older, she'd started to doubt her mother's explanation that their father had been called away on an important work assignment, one that prevented him from communicating with them (Military spy? Space explorer? Mad scientist?), but it was better than the alternatives, so she left that explanation in place, like a poster covering a cracked wall.

As for all the other stories, Amber didn't believe that her mother believed in the fanciful things she told them: the witch and the fairies and the magical creatures that randomly popped up in conversation; the rare purple-tailed squirrel; the French-speaking spider-bird. Instead, Amber had recently decided that her mother said these things because regular life—the driving to and from school, the raising of children, the hourly jobs, the never-ending battle to get people to civically engage—was just so very, very boring.

Sandra had told Amber that she used to dream of doing Great Things—pronounced with a special emphasis like Engaged Citizen. Before meeting Amber and Beetle's father, she'd backpacked in South America and canvassed for Greenpeace and marched for human rights. So if these made-up stories were what Sandra needed to keep herself entertained so she wouldn't give up the only long-term job title she'd ever held—that of mother of Amber and Beetle—then Amber would play by the rules for as long as she needed to, keeping her eye rolls and aggravated sighs to a minimum and letting her mother have her fun.

That plan had worked. Until today.

Because it became clear as their rusted station wagon passed the Parallel's building on their way home from school—and their mother didn't remind them to wave hello, or even glance at their parallel selves—that something was wrong. Terribly wrong. Beetle's hand froze in a half-wave. He wore a worried expression, like an actor waiting on another actor who'd missed a cue.

"Aren't you going to say something?" Amber demanded.

"Say something about what, dear?"

Her mother's eyes were firmly locked on the car in front of them.

It was like one of the few math problems Amber had gotten right on the earlier test. If her mother did not say anything about the Parallels—and her mother *always* said something about the Parallels—then this person could not be her mother.

Amber ruled out a head injury. The ability to recognize her children and drive a car and nod along to the radio announcer seemed to suggest Sandra was right as mud. (Oh, Amber, your mother has been an influence; the cliché is right as rain.) This meant her mother had somehow been swapped with this look-alike, sound-alike person. And if that was the case, then it was one hundred percent, without question, Amber's fault.

3

After they'd parked in front of their apartment building—a building as old and crumbling as the Towel Service—the woman who was so clearly not Amber and Beetle's mother said, "Kids, bring in the bags, please."

Amber and Beetle went to the trunk of the car. Two grocery bags overflowed with vegetables and fruits and something wrapped in white paper.

Strange thing number ten (or are we up to eleven?): their mother only ever made pasta for dinner. Her idea of variety was to cook up different shapes—long noodles, short noodles, those funny curly ones—and rotate between butter and tomato sauce. But it was still pasta. Always. Occasionally, she'd throw in things for "added nutrition": broccoli or tofu, canned olives or peas, and once she added pineapple (it's not as bad as it sounds). Amber and Beetle traded a look as they carried the bags up the walk.

In the apartment Sandra said, "Take your shoes off; I just vacuumed."

Did they even own a vacuum? But then Amber and Beetle were hit with the biggest surprise of all. After kicking their shoes off as instructed, they carried the bags into the kitchen. Sandra set her own bag down and removed her hat, but instead of The Nest tumbling down her back, her hair drifted like dandelion fluff into a straight, brushed bob that barely reached her shoulders.

"What happened to your hair?" Beetle asked. Likely, the most words he had strung together all day.

"Much better, don't you think? Took the hairdresser over an hour."

Amber couldn't hold it in anymore. "You're not our mother!"

She ran into her room and slammed the door, releasing the tears that had been building all day. Of all the problems she'd experienced with her classes and friends and Sandra's earlier oddness, this was the absolute worst. Her mother's crazy, curly, knotted hair. How could it be gone?

Amber had a theory about why her mother had not cut her hair for nearly ten years (other than a snipping of ends when it turned to mat), and it had nothing to do with style or laziness. It was instead based on a casual comment her mother had made years ago to Amber's question of "won't you ever get it cut?" Sandra had gotten a faraway look and responded, "Funny, the last time I did was the day before your father left." That offhand remark had lodged itself in Amber's mind as cause and effect. Father returns. Mother cuts hair. That clearly hadn't happened, although just to make sure, Amber sucked back a sob and listened for a male voice. Instead she heard a quiet rapping at the door. A Beetle knock.

"Don't come in!"

She leaned against the door and that's when she noticed the pile of neatly folded shirts on her bed, next to a pile of neatly folded pants and socks rolled into balls. Seeing this made her get all teary again. The clean laundry—itself a rare occurrence—was always dumped on the bench in her mother's room. If you needed something, you went in and dug around. Clothes were never separated. Or folded. Socks reunited only if you stuck your hand in the pile and, with random luck, pulled out two that matched.

The rapping came again followed by Beetle's soft voice. "Please, Amber."

She dried her face on a clean shirt and tossed it on the floor, then cracked the door. Her brother looked even paler and smaller than usual. She opened the door wide enough for him to pass through.

"Amber, she's making chicken for dinner."

At this point nothing surprised Amber, and that included the announcement that their vegetarian mother—who made them take a moment of silence when spotting a dead animal on the side of the road, who spoke to birds as if they were neighbors, who signed every internet petition arguing for animal rights and had started a few of her own—would be preparing poultry.

"Do you really think she's not our mom?" Beetle looked at Amber as if he hoped she'd laugh and say *Don't be silly.*

Instead, Amber nodded. She felt like she was done crying. Her tear ducts were probably empty anyway. "I'll figure this out, Little Bug," she said. That's what she called Beetle when he was being a pest. Today she used it to add a dash of normality to their otherwise crazy day. "Why don't you go offer to help. Let me know if she says anything else weird. I need to do some thinking."

He nodded and disappeared out the door. Amber picked up her stuffed lion and started to pace. She always thought better when she paced. "So, Lion," she said. "We have ourselves a perplexing situation."

Amber liked to use big words while pacing. It made her feel as if she were more capable of making Big Decisions. And she was proud of her vocabulary, which came from her second favorite pastime after softball: reading. (Although learning words through books did sometimes lead to mispronunciations. "You-surp dear, not uh-surp," Ms. Mac, her social studies teacher, had corrected when Amber tried to show off a new word the other day. "But good usage.") Amber's mother was a self-proclaimed bookworm and some of the nicest times Amber could remember were when she'd curled up in her mother's bed, each of them engrossed in a book, worlds away, yet sharing the warm burrow of her mother's faded blue comforter.

Amber looked into Lion's eyes, which were brown plastic, but an attentive brown plastic.

"We need to address three basic questions: Why did this happen? Where is Sandra? How do we get things back to the way they were?"

In her head, Lion answered. "That first one is easy. You got what you wished for."

Amber tossed him onto the bed and followed, her face finally meeting the softness of the pillow. Yes, Lion was right. That morning—which already seemed so long ago it could have been a different decade—Amber had reached a breaking point. They'd been having a typically crazy time trying to get out the door, even though Amber had told her mother for the gazillionth time that she needed to get to school early. She thought maybe she could find Debbie alone—since Debbie always arrived first—and ask, "Are you mad at me?" Sandra, who didn't fully emerge from sleep until sometime after noon, had seemed especially flighty, doubling back for her car key—she claimed it best to keep it separate from her house keys because if the witch grabbed one, she'd still have the other—then for her phone, and then because she might have left the stove on. "Just a minute, just a minute," she said, right before she spilled a cup of coffee down the front of her shirt. "Bartleby James!" This was Sandra's favorite curse. Amber had no idea where it came from, but it was certainly better than the alternatives Sandra used when she thought they were out of earshot. Then after cleaning up, she lost her car key again.

"Oh well," Sandra said. "Guess the witch has it in for us today."

Amber exploded. "It's not the witch's fault! It's your fault! It's always your fault! I wish you were just a normal mother!" Then she'd stormed down the stairs.

When Amber's mother exited the building with her spare key, phone, and a clean(ish) shirt, she'd been her usual chatty, strange self. But at some point on the drive, the transformation had taken place. If only Amber hadn't been too busy pouting, she might have noticed the switch. That would help answer the Where. As for the Why, she had to consider that one of her mother's crazy tales was actually true. Could there have been some mischievous fairy lurking nearby, waiting for someone to blurt out a wish? Or the fairy godmother, back on the clock? If so, that would mean that the short-haired woman in the kitchen, making chicken for dinner, and looking all neat and put together, and not talking about witches or parallel friends, really was their mother, just an altered version of her. Or maybe it was nothing more than a performance? Her mother putting on an act. But Amber knew that there were things her mother would never do, even to prove a point: get a haircut, cook chicken.

Which meant, as Lion said, Amber had gotten exactly what she'd wished for.

"Amber, come set the table," the woman in the kitchen called.

4

On her way to the kitchen, Amber stopped in the bathroom to splash water on her face. She checked her reflection in the mirror: wide-eyed, pale, her hair sprung loose from her ponytail. "It will all be fine," she said, although she felt like a bad actor, just saying the lines but not believing them to be true.

The kitchen smelled like real cooking: garlic and onions sizzled in a pan, bread warmed in the oven. Something that did indeed look like raw poultry was on the cutting board.

Sandra wore a faded blue and white apron tied over her clothes that she must have found in the back of a drawer. She'd used one of Amber's ponytail holders to draw her hair into a bun that jutted like the clipped tail of their other neighbor, Mrs. Sanchez's, miniature schnauzer.

"Amber, there you are. Please set the table and bring your lunch box to the sink. There should be enough here for you to have chicken salad tomorrow."

Sandra glanced at the ceiling above the kitchen table, almost as if she were expecting something to appear, but perhaps it was to look away from the sliced onion, which made Amber's eyes water even though she wasn't near it.

The lunch box was in her backpack by the front door. Amber checked the inside to make sure it wasn't wet, which might lead to a conversation she didn't want to have about spilled water bottles, and saw the slip of paper. She'd forgotten about the note. Not only did it still seem odd, but it seemed especially odd given the way their mother/non-mother was behaving. She stuck it in the pocket of her jeans, grateful there'd been no water damage.

Beetle walked out of the kitchen and grabbed his backpack.

"Hey, Bug, did you get one of Sandra's notes today?"

"Didn't make sense." He held his backpack upside down. Out fell crumpled homework, a twisted pair of swim goggles, and loose playing cards, along with his lunch box.

"Quick, give it to me."

He opened his lunch box (a green one with The Incredible Hulk) and handed her the note. She flicked off a piece of apple and added the note to her pocket.

After bringing her lunch box to the sink, Amber took out silverware and plates, trying to select the ones with the least number of chips. The kitchen table had been cleared. She couldn't remember the last time she'd seen the entire surface. It was usually covered with unread mail and magazines and her mother's papers. They'd eat in small clearings surrounded by the piles, like cubicle walls. But it seemed that in between the haircut and grocery shopping and the laundry, this mother had found time to do that too.

After the table was set, Amber said, "I have to start on homework." She gave Beetle a little push.

"Me too. I have homework."

"Okay. Let me know if you need any help."

And another strange occurence! Amber was done trying to count. Their mother never offered to help with homework. She never even asked if they had any and always seemed surprised when their report cards arrived with decent grades (even Amber's math grade, although she had to put in a lot of effort to get it to a B) as if they'd managed to sneak in their learning behind her back.

Amber led Beetle to her room and told him to close the door. She unfolded the notes and placed them side by side. Hers still made no sense. *The witch warns of strange weather. Hope your mother has an umbrella.*

"Like Mary Poppins?" Beetle suggested, after leaning in to read it.

Amber flashed on an image of their real mother coasting

through the window to rescue them from this imposter. No, there must be something they weren't getting. A clue within a clue.

She read Beetle's. *The witch wants you to know you can walk through it.* That made even less sense. First off, the witch again. And walk through what? Amber had learned never to use a pronoun without an identifying noun. (This reminded her to look around for her English book. She saw it under her chair but would still forget to put it in her backpack.)

"What do you think?" Beetle asked.

He'd pulled at his hair so much that it pouffed over his head. Usually he did this during thunderstorms or when their mother left them home alone for too long.

"I think I need a walk-it," Amber said.

A walk-it was what their mother advised whenever they had a problem they couldn't figure out. One of the few cases where Sandra seemed to have the right idea, and Amber took walk-its all the time: when faced with a difficult math problem, or when she needed to come up with a paper topic, but also sometimes when Beetle was being annoying or Sandra was making her mad. She had a path she liked to follow: down to the park, around the block, and sometimes, if she needed a few extra minutes, another turn around the building. A walk-it often gave her new ways of coming at a problem, or, at the very least, a better attitude. She checked her watch. It wasn't quite six. Sandra wouldn't have even started boiling water yet. But as she went to the front door to get her shoes, the woman who was not quite her mother announced, "Dinner."

The meal earned its title. Beetle asked for thirds, and Amber ate every bite, although in her head she apologized (and then apologized again) to the chicken. After dinner they had to help clean up. Then Amber was told it was too dark to walk, even though it was just before dusk, which Sandra had taught them was the best time to go. "Magic Hour," she'd called it. And because she always had to make everything even weirder: "The time of day when our world and other worlds overlap."

"I'll just take a quick one. Like I do all the time!"

Amber hadn't meant to shout. For some reason, since turning twelve, she'd lost control of her volume settings and things that should be said at a regular level came out as a roar. When this happened her mother would yell back, as if entering a contest, the Who-Could-get-Aggravated-the-Fastest contest with both of them ending with strained voices.

But today, this mother said in a firm but even tone, "I said no. And what about homework? I doubt you got much done earlier without your backpack."

Amber kicked her shoes off so they smacked against the wall. She slammed into her room, forgot her backpack, slammed back out to get it, and gave one last slam for good measure.

There was a knock a few minutes later.

"I'm about to serve dessert." The mother's voice was still firm but not unkind. "If you apologize for the racket, you're welcome to join us. We're having apple pie."

Apple pie? They had that only at Thanksgiving when their mother bowed to tradition with a trip to Baker's Square. Sandra believed too much sugar corroded (her word) their brains and that a piece of fruit made a perfectly acceptable dessert. Every now and then, when they'd had a rough week, Sandra would shout, "All for one and one for ice cream," and surprise them with a carton she'd bought at the store. That was fun, even though the ice cream would be made from some nondairy ingredient like coconut milk or almonds. But Amber wasn't going to apologize. Not even for apple pie. This mother was being so unreasonable in her reasonableness. Beetle was probably on his second piece and it was all just so unfair. Amber was starting to think that normal mothers were worse than abnormal ones.

After struggling through her math homework, Amber read for a while and then went to bed. She wanted to shut out the day, but without the walk-it all the thoughts that had been piling up swirled like fragments in a snow globe. What should she do if she woke up tomorrow and this wasn't all a bad dream? Should she confront this mother? She'd probably just be dismissed, or laughed at, or worse, get sent to the pediatrician, Dr. Don, who had warts and terrible breath. (Their mother found him entertaining, and claimed he was like a character "straight out of Dickens.") Should Amber confess to Beetle about the wish she'd made? Maybe Beetle preferred this new mother who shopped and fed and cared for them in an orderly fashion. Now that she looked so presentable, maybe she'd get a normal job. Maybe looking so boring (and, yes, this mother did look bland in that hairdo) meant she wouldn't mind being bored every now and again. No more made-up stories. No more fairies and witches and parallel lands.

Amber wondered if she'd prefer that too. It was so quiet right now. Usually her mother was banging around and knocking things over and shouting, "Bartleby James!" And how nice it was to go to sleep without the lingering smell of something burned from dinner, including strands of their mother's hair. This woman was still their mother. Only her behavior had changed (well, that and her hairstyle, and her values about animals). And really, how certain could Amber be about the Why? Was her association any more legitimate than that silly rhyme "Step on a crack, break your mother's back"? But sleep would be far better than having to consider the biggest question on the list: Where? Because if somehow that wasn't their actual mother in the kitchen, then where was she? Was she worried about them? Was she safe? Was she scared?

After tossing and turning and knocking her pillow to the floor multiple times, Amber drifted off. She dreamed she was on her way to school when she saw Sandra, long hair streaming, waving from the side of the road. "Stop," Amber yelled. "Stop the car!" But her new mother said, "You can't be late for school." Then she heard snickering and saw that Clara and Debbie were in the back seat with poor Beetle crushed in between. They pointed out the window at Sandra and shouted, "Look at that woman. What a freak. Be gone, freak. Be gone." Amber heard herself shout "No!" She woke with her heart pounding.

It was still night. Hearing a whimper, she peered into the dark and saw Beetle curled at the foot of the bed like a pet dog. She kicked at the covers, more out of a need to shake herself from the dream than with an intent to do harm. He whimpered again.

"What are you doing, Little Bug? Go creep back to your own room."

"I can't sleep," he said, although his voice sounded half asleep. "Can you tell me one of Mom's stories?"

Amber could have continued her kicking attack, but she had to admit it was nice to have company. "People one or animal one?"

"People," he yawned. "But maybe an animal too. A furry one. No chickens."

So Amber lay back on her pillow and tried, to the best of her imagination, to channel one of their mother's nighttime tales.

"Once upon a time there was a crazy old wizard and an even crazier old witch," she began. By the time she got to the part about the spelling competition to win the prize of the cutest talking panda bear in all of magic land, she could tell that Beetle was asleep. Because he was taking up the bottom half of her bed, she rolled into her own Beetle-like ball and allowed the rest of the story to unfold in her imagination. In that way it was as if her mother had lulled her to sleep too.

5

The next day of school was even worse. For once, they were out the door on time and arrived early. But all that meant was Amber had to kill time at her locker while Clara, Debbie, and Leanne whispered on the other side of the hall. There was the forgotten English book (again!), plus the math test came back with a note, *Amber, please see me before lunch.* There was also a handout about a parent/child field trip on Saturday to a dairy farm outside of town. She stuffed the flyer into the pocket of her jeans. Any mention of a parent-involved public activity made Amber cringe in anticipated embarrassment, even though it occurred to her that it might be less of an embarrassment to have this new shorter-haired mother along.

When she finally reached the lunchroom, the girls at her regular table had piled their backpacks onto the extra seat, so she went to the other seventh grade girls' lunch table and saw an empty seat next to Sarika. Sarika was new that year. Amber had never really talked to her. Clara's mother had sold Sarika's family their house, closer to the part of town where Amber lived. Clara said they'd moved from another country; she couldn't remember the name, but it was where people ate cats and didn't have plumbing and their food smelled weird.

"Can I sit here?" Amber asked.

Sarika nodded. Her hair was tucked into two tidy braids and she wore jeans and a T-shirt, like most of the other kids. Amber snuck a look at Sarika's lunch. It appeared to be a hummus wrap (the type that Amber had hoped to make), chips, and a chocolate chip cookie. Nothing remotely cat-like. Or smelly. And chips *and* a cookie! Amber was envious. Opening her own lunch, she'd forgotten she wouldn't find a cheese sandwich. The lumpy chicken salad made her think of the stories Sandra had told them about what went on at poultry plants. She pushed it aside. Also in the lunch box: carrot sticks, fruit snacks (Sandra considered these to be merely fruit impersonators), and, yes, even a small bag of chocolate chip cookies. Underneath the cookies Amber spotted a piece of folded paper. Could it be another clue? She grabbed it and held it in her hand, the way she might delay unwrapping the paper on a surprise gift. Eagerness won out. She unfolded the paper and read in neatly spaced print, Please be prompt. Amber wadded the note and put it with the chicken salad, both destined for the trash. She would have gladly traded the fruit snacks and the cookies for one of her mother's silly scribbled notes.

A shriek of laughter. She looked at the other table and saw Debbie and Clara laughing with their heads tipped back. The other girls followed a beat late, then leaned forward like a wave to gather any word, smile, or gesture from the two girls in the center.

"Seems like we missed the joke," Sarika said. Her voice was soft, with a lilt that made Amber think of music.

From this vantage point, the table theatrics looked like the joke. Amber wished she had the courage to admit to her lunch partner that nothing Debbie and Clara said was ever that amusing.

After lunch, Amber walked with Sarika toward their lockers. Leanne and Clara pushed by, wrinkling their noses. Amber hoped Sarika didn't notice.

On Thursdays, Amber had art class in the afternoon. Her assigned seat was next to Debbie's. Usually the teacher, Ms. Codell, would tell them to stop giggling and get back to work. Today, Amber expected Debbie wouldn't even acknowledge her presence, but when Amber sat down, Debbie leaned over. "Isn't Sarika so weird?"

Amber felt her smile emerge against her will. She couldn't

deny that it made her feel good to have Debbie's attention again. Still, not speaking up to defend Sarika made her feel equally bad. Debbie winked. She winked back. A Pavlovian response, something else she'd learned in science. Although she'd never before considered if Debbie's friendship was a worthy reward.

ও

At the end of the day, Amber followed the note's command, found Beetle at his locker, and ordered him to "hustle it up, Little Bug." Good thing, too. Yet again, the car was in front of the line. Clara and Debbie didn't even look at her when she walked by, as if she were some kid from a different grade. On the way home, Amber had to answer the same questions about school. She didn't mention the math test, and she definitely wasn't going to bring up her friend issue.

"They seem unimaginative," Sandra had said at the end of last year, which was pretty much the worst insult Amber's mother could give. Sandra also labeled them over-consumers who "don't appreciate the spoils they've been given."

Over the summer Debbie and Clara would be attending an overnight camp out of state. When they'd told Amber about their plans, she'd said, "Sounds fun. Maybe I'll look into it."

Clara had offered an apologetic smile. "Well, you know, it's really expensive. Even my parents are complaining about how much it costs."

Translation: *Sorry, you're too poor to go.*

It wasn't like it was a big secret that Amber and Beetle were scholarship kids. It just made Amber want to work harder to prove she belonged there, but whenever Debbie and Clara reminded her of her status, she felt like someone had taken a knife to a sandwich, separating the superfluous crust (her) from the desirable center part with all the fixings (her friends).

Amber asked her mother about the camp anyway.

"Phooey," Sandra had said. "There's nothing wrong with the Y camp. It's all the same. You swim, you play sports, you stay outside long enough to get mosquito bites and a tan." Seeing Amber's glum expression, she added, "I know exactly what you need and it's not any overpriced camp. You need a dance-out!" She'd put a disco CD into an old boom box, as battered as their car, and dragged Amber into the middle of the living room. "Say it with me," she'd shouted over the music. "It just doesn't matter! It just doesn't matter!" Amber tried to keep the pout, but it really did work: dancing to disco while shouting this mantra was like a magical remedy; or as her mother liked to say, "Some disco today keeps the doctor away!" Even Beetle got into it, doing his own move that Sandra called the Beetle Shimmy.

Amber tried to imagine the nicely put-together woman in the driver's seat suggesting a dance-out. She couldn't. It was as difficult as imagining her actual mother getting her hair cut or showing up on time or making chicken. On the way to school that morning, this mother had again driven past the familiar sites without a flicker of acknowledgment. She'd ignored the witch house and the fairy garden, and when the spray-painted van zoomed by, all she did was sigh and say, "Terrible driver." Now, as they neared the School Towel Service building, Amber decided to try a more overt test.

"Hello, Parallels," she said and waved broadly. She turned to the back seat and gave Beetle a look so he would do the same.

"How's it going, Parallels?" he said, with an equally large motion.

"Why are you waving like that?" the mother said.

Amber didn't respond. As she looked out the window she made two surprising observations.

One: the mother in the reflected glass of the School Towel Service building appeared to have long flowing hair.

Two: Even though the weather was beautiful—another

sunny, cloudless day—the sky reflected in the School Towel Service window was dull gray. And although Amber couldn't be one hundred percent certain, it sure did look like the wipers on the reflected vehicle swished across a windshield streaked with rain.

6

"Beetle, come here." Amber motioned him into her room. Beetle moved quickly. Likely because Amber had invited him into her room more times in the past two days than the entire previous year. If he ever tried to enter without an invitation, the visits ended with objects (mostly soft, unless there was a book in Amber's reach) hitting him in the back as he fled.

In the kitchen the mother was chopping vegetables. She'd informed them when they got home from school that they'd be dining on stir-fry (since when did they "dine"?), but that it would take her time to prepare.

"Have to get vegetables into those growing bodies of yours." She'd smiled and ruffled Beetle's hair.

Beetle had scurried away. Their real mother would have known that he loathed anyone's hands in his hair.

Amber paced as Beetle leaned against her bed. "When we drove by the Parallels, did you notice anything unusual?"

Beetle scrunched his face. That was his thinking look. "It was dark."

"Not dark," Amber corrected. "Raining."

He shrugged and picked up a foam softball that Amber used when she wanted to practice indoors. She pulled it from his hand.

"Like in my note. Remember it said something about needing an umbrella. I think we need to take a walk-it. Go get your homework done and then come back here. We'll need to leave before *Mother* says it's too late." Amber decided she'd keep that sarcastic tone when describing the not-quite version of her mother. Although, truthfully, this tone wasn't all that different from the one she'd used on the many occasions *Sandra* had gotten on her nerves.

&

This time, Amber and Beetle got away without issue, most likely because they were already sprinting out the door when Amber yelled, "Takingawalkitbye."

The sun had started to dip and the air had cooled. They zipped their jackets as Amber took them on a route she'd mapped in her mind. They walked the first block in silence. Beetle veered side to side to scatter the leaves. Amber felt surprisingly calm. This could be any night. People walked their dogs. Kids rode bikes. Rush-hour traffic crept along. It could have been a week ago, their real mother at home, letting the pasta water boil over while she'd lectured them on voting rights. The memory made Amber's throat tighten.

"Where?" Beetle asked as Amber crossed another block instead of turning to the left for their usual circle back home.

Yes, Amber thought. *That is exactly the question.* "We have the note about the umbrella," she said. Beetle nodded. "And I said it looked like it was raining when we drove by the Parallels' building today." He nodded again. "Well, hear me out, because I'm about to spin one of Sandra's wacky tales. What if her story about the parallel world isn't just some made-up thing? What if she got swapped with the Parallel's mother and that's what the note meant? That she would need an umbrella because it's raining there. Somehow she was able to get us a hint."

But, Amber asked herself, how would the notes have gotten in their lunch boxes after they were already at school?

And more questions arose. If their mother wanted to give them a message, why not just state it outright? Why put it in some obscure riddle about the witch? Perhaps Amber had just imagined the rain in the School Towel Service window because her subconscious wanted it to be there. And yet, wasn't this exactly the kind of thing their mother would have encouraged? Be open-minded. Use your imagination.

Beetle voiced her first question. "How would she know to give us the notes if she didn't get swapped with the other mother until after we'd left home?"

This led Amber to worry that if the exchange had happened, maybe it was because their mother wanted to get away. Could she have needed an adventure that badly? Did she think this would be like taking a vacation, while leaving a perfectly suitable (one might even argue, more suitable) babysitter in her place? Amber walked faster, as if trying to escape a smelly trash can or growling dog. As if she could outrun this thought. She noticed that, without intending to, she had spaced her steps to avoid the cracks on the sidewalk.

Beetle broke into a jog to keep up. "Do you think she knew this was going to happen?"

Amber jumped to avoid a larger crack. "Maybe if we find her, she'll explain."

Beetle's eyes grew wide. Amber hadn't meant to say *if* they'd find her. She'd meant the *if* to be about their mother's willingness to share an explanation, but her nerves had jumbled her speech. They *had* to find her. There was no other option. The woman in Amber and Beetle's kitchen making a fancy stir-fry was a perfectly fine mother, but she wasn't Sandra. She wasn't *their* mother. Amber understood this with full clarity. All Amber wanted now was to tell her real mother—the crazy-haired, daydreaming, doesn't-give-a-hoot-about-what-other-people-think,won't-shut-up-about political-activism mother—what had happened since her disappearance. She wanted to hear her mother say, "It just doesn't matter" and pull her into a hug.

When was the last time Amber had let her mother hug her? A month ago? More? The worry grew. What if this wasn't just an adventure? What if their mother had her own wish to trade for a set of more imaginative children? Children who didn't roll their eyes. Children who hugged. If so, then the only thing Amber could hope for was that Sandra had also found the match not to her liking. "The grass is always greener on the other side of the river," her mother liked to say.

Amber and Beetle reached the final intersection. Across the street, halfway down the block, Amber could make out the faint white letters for School Towel Service on the crumbling brick. She was acting on a hunch, which she hoped was right. It had to be right. She checked the sky. The sun had dropped farther down. There wasn't much time. The streetlight changed to green and the walk sign came on, but their purpose was far too important to walk. Grabbing Beetle's hand, she ran into the street.

"Come on, Beetle! Let's find Mother."

7

Now what?

Amber stood with Beetle in front of the darkened window. Up close there was nothing to suggest that their reflections weren't a perfect match. The Amber and Beetle in the window wore the same outfits, their hair blew the same way in the breeze, and with the fading light it was hard to tell if the weather was any different. Although there were some shadows that could be puddles on the mirrored version of the sidewalk.

Amber waved. Her reflection waved too.

"Beetle, do something silly," she instructed.

They shook their bodies. Jumped. Shimmied. Their reflections in the window matched their moves perfectly. The sky provided a pink-hued backdrop as Magic Hour approached. She must have been desperate to buy into her mother's made-up story about overlapping worlds. What had she expected? That they'd show up here, and all of a sudden their mother would emerge from the doorway shouting, "What took you so long?"

But Amber wasn't ready to give up. In the books she read, and the stories her mother told, it was all about believing. Amber said with as much conviction as she could muster, "At Magic Hour, worlds overlap." She repeated it silently, working her brain muscle as hard as she could. *I believe in Magic Hour. I believe it's true. I believe in Magic Hour. I believe it's true.*

Still nothing.

Think! she ordered. She felt like she was missing something. Had they forgotten a clue?

"Beetle, what did your note say? Something about walking

through it, right?" Beetle and his reflection nodded. "Maybe the *it* was this building."

Amber walked past the window to a recessed area with a large black door. The concrete was littered with old newspapers and broken glass, cobwebs hung in every corner, and a terrible smell rose from the pavement. Amber wrinkled her nose in disgust. It smelled just like the time her team had to use the boys' restroom at an away game. The door looked as if it hadn't been opened in years, but she grabbed the metal handle and pushed. She pulled. She pushed again as hard as she could, as if it were the door's fault that she was out of ideas. She returned to the sidewalk, prepared to tell Beetle it was time to give up and go home, when she saw him place his hand through the glass and step forward.

"Beetle!"

She ran toward him, then stopped. While Beetle's figure disappeared in one direction, another Beetle appeared, as if stepping through the glass from the inside. This other Beetle looked around, saw her, and sprinted down the street in the direction of their apartment.

"Beetle!" she called again. Her first instinct was to chase after him, but she paused at the window. Her solo reflection looked back, but something seemed off. She took a step back. So did the Amber in the mirror. Took a step closer. Same. She studied the face. It was the expression. Amber had never once held her lips in that type of pinched line and certainly wasn't doing it now. It made her look haughty, like she was holding back a laugh at her own expense. The last gleam of pink exploded in the sky, flashing over her head into the glass, but instead of refracting, it spread out before her, lighting a path ahead, as if the glass weren't there.

Amber put out her hand. It met no resistance. She swung her leg over the bottom of the window frame and stepped through.

Part Two: There

8

Amber stood on a street. It appeared to be the same street she'd just come from. She took a step and water soaked her tennis shoe. A puddle. She looked up. Dark clouds she hadn't noticed earlier scuttled past.

"Beetle!" Amber shouted.

She seemed to be alone, other than a few cars driving by. She looked at the window and put her hand on the glass. Solid. Her reflection's expression matched what she thought was her own: dumbfounded, uncertain, as if demanding that her image answer the question, *What now?*

"Beetle!" she called again, but then she remembered seeing him—or at least a version of him—running toward home. Perhaps that's what she should do. She hadn't thought this through enough. Where did she think she'd end up? Inside the building, surrounded by old washing machines? Her mother tied up in a corner, patiently awaiting a rescue?

With no other ideas, Amber headed home. The more she walked, the more it felt like the game in which two almost identical pictures were placed side by side and the object was to circle the oddities. Wings attached to a baseball cap. A shirt with one less stripe. Here, she had to dig through her memory to recreate the setting. Didn't this block usually have a light instead of a stop sign? Didn't Lee Street have a crosswalk? Some of the houses seemed different, but maybe it was just the cloudy sky that made them look so dreary, or the secretive aspect of seeing so many shuttered windows. Amber felt off-kilter in a way that suggested there were other inconsistencies. That's when she noticed the light was odd, hazy with a grayish-yellow hue, like a photograph that had been overexposed. Her movements felt odd too, as if she were walking at a slant even though, as far as she could see, the sidewalk stretched flat before her. The street was empty except for a passing white bus.

A few blocks from home she spotted Beetle. He'd slowed to a walk.

"Wait up, Little Bug," she called.

He stopped and turned. He was breathing heavily.

She had never seen him so happy to see her.

"Why did you run away like that?" She sounded crosser than she meant to.

"I waited," he said. "But you didn't come."

"You didn't wait," she said, still sounding bossy and cross. "I saw you running. And it only took me a minute before I got—" She paused. Got in? Got across? Got through? She couldn't get her head around where they were. Were they actually inside that building, like the world of Horton's Whos, oblivious on their clover fluff; or were they orbiting through space on a whole different planet? Or maybe they were still home, and it was her memory that was all wrong. She felt shaky, thrown by the light and the slant, as if at any moment she might pitch forward. She looked for something to ground her and saw the familiar street signs. Ridge. Main. "—before I followed you."

Beetle shook his head. "Not true." His face scrunched like he was fighting back tears. This was a different scrunch than his thinking scrunch. It was the one he made when he was sure he was right but no one believed him.

She tried to check her watch but the light hurt her eyes, and she couldn't make it out.

A man in a suit walked toward them, staring at his phone. He almost plowed into Beetle. "Sorry," he said.

His eyes flickered over their heads. Amber thought he was checking the sky for rain. But following his eye line she saw a security camera, posted on a lamppost, pointed in their direction.

"You should hurry," he said. "You'll be late for dinner." He walked past them, eyes back on his phone.

Amber picked up her pace, forcing Beetle to trot along. As they turned onto their block, she was surprised by her relief at seeing their apartment building, a place that usually brought nothing but embarrassment. The entryway had a yellowish glow. Had the building manager finally fixed the light fixture? No. The lighting seemed to come from the sky, which splashed its washed-out yellow over the entry, the sidewalk, the bars on the first-floor windows, an empty flower box.

On any other day, Amber would have cycled through her knowledge to try to remember if she'd ever seen the sky that color before, and what the different colors meant about precipitation, but right now all she cared about was finding their real mother. What if they walked in and there was already another Amber there? Another Beetle? What if it wasn't Sandra after all? Maybe, like Beetle, she'd gotten tired of waiting and had already gone somewhere else, another giant step away.

Amber grabbed Beetle by the wrist and pulled him to a stop. "We need code words," she said. "A way to make sure that I'm me and you're you. Just in case there are more of us."

"I could be ice cream," Beetle said. He really loved ice cream. Even the coconut kind.

"Too common. We need something that only we would know. How about 'The Parallels'?"

Beetle shrugged. "Wouldn't they know? I mean, we always say, 'Hello, Parallels.'"

"Good point."

It started to rain. Amber stepped under the narrow overhang to stay dry. With that movement she had it. "The witch," she said. "That's mine. And yours can be Mr. Zagoom. That's how we'll know."

If she'd been paying better attention, she might have seen

the light shift, a blink's worth of white infusing the yellow. She pulled on the door; the lock thankfully seemed to be broken in this world too. As they walked up the stairs to the apartment landing, her stomach felt as if it contained a million flying insects all chirping, *What if? What if?* But, no, she had to think positively. Or, as her mother always said, hope for the best but be prepared for good enough. As she reached for the doorknob, she put on her best brave smile.

"Welcome to our home away from home."

9

"Children, is that you?"

It sounded like Sandra's voice. Although so did the voice of the woman they'd left behind. The voice came from the living room, not the kitchen. A good sign.

But then the voice said, "You barely made it back in time. You need to be more careful."

Amber heard a sharpness that she couldn't remember ever hearing in her mother's voice.

They took their shoes off (the other mother's rules having taken hold) and rounded the corner to find this mother sitting in the floral armchair by the bookcase. Long hair fell down her back in all its brown and gray curly splendor (check); she wore jeans and a button-down shirt (check, although the button-down was fitted and the jeans had no holes); and she was reading a book (triple check).

"Mother?" Amber asked cautiously, scared she'd reveal a secret by using her mother's proper name. "What are we having for dinner?"

The woman in the chair offered an apologetic smile. "Pasta again, I'm afraid."

Amber's shoulders relaxed for the first time in what seemed like forever. Her voice shook. "You would not believe," she said, "how much I was hoping that's what you'd say." She was about to run over and fling herself into her mother's lap when a buzzer, like a school bell, went off.

Her mother rose, knocking the book to the floor.

The chair, cleared of her mother's figure, was in surprisingly good condition. No wine stain in the center cushion, no stuffing popping through the top corner. Amber wanted to investigate the room further but her mother's sharp tone returned.

"We'd better hurry. Amber, set the table. Beetle, wash your hands; they're filthy. No more walks if you can't be prompt."

The flying insects renewed their flapping. Amber followed into the kitchen and opened the cabinet where they stored the dishes. The plates were similar to theirs but without chips or cracks. Some even matched. While she put down the place settings, her mother took a pot out of the refrigerator and set it on the stove.

"I lost track of time too. We might have to eat pasta *froid* tonight," she said. "That's French for cold. I'd planned to start when you got back, but you were so late."

This time her tone sounded almost accusatory.

"So we'll eat when it's heated," Amber said. "No big deal."

Their mother (Amber was fairly certain it was their mother) didn't respond, just spooned the congealed pasta onto their plates. She took a bag of string beans from the freezer and poured them next to the pasta. That wasn't unusual; both Amber and Beetle preferred them frozen.

"Sit," she said.

Sandra glanced up to the corner of the room. Her glance mimicked the man on the street. That's when Amber noticed the egg-shaped object hanging from the ceiling. It was white like the walls and would have blended in except for a small red light flashing on top. It made her think of a fancy smoke detector, or one of the voice-activated devices that Clara and Debbie had in their houses that played music and changed channels on the TV. But then a dinger sounded, the light turned green, and the egg cracked opened to reveal what looked like a camera lens.

"Eat," their mother stage-whispered. In a louder voice she said, "Amber, tell me about your day at school."

Amber had been about to stick a string bean in her mouth and wasn't sure which took priority, the order to eat or to answer the question (something told her that answering the question while eating was not the right choice).

"It was fine," she replied.

Her mother's eyes flickered again toward the camera, then back at Amber with an imploring look. Amber thought harder; her day at school, as terrible as it had been, seemed like weeks ago.

"I...uh...got my math test back today and...um...I ate lunch with the new girl. Well, she's not really new anymore, just since the beginning of the year."

Sandra nodded although she didn't seem to be listening. "Bernard, tell me about your day."

Beetle had been trying to pierce a piece of cold pasta. When he didn't look up, Amber kicked him under the table.

"What?" he asked.

Amber whispered out of the side of her mouth. "She means you, *Bernard.* Talk about your day."

Beetle scowled. "It was okay." The pasta catapulted off his plate and onto Amber's. He giggled.

Amber kicked him again, harder. They heard another dinging sound. The egg lens closed and the light went back to red.

From the counter a tablet buzzed as the screen lit up. Sandra sighed and went to retrieve it, but she was diverted when the pasta sauce exploded out of the pot, splattering the stove, floor, and ceiling.

"Bartleby James!" Sandra shouted.

Amber fetched a rag without being asked. With each new check mark, she felt a sense of relief, which was countered by her mother's mood and these strange technologies. (Although how often she'd wished for a tablet instead of the old laptop her mother had, which could barely get online.)

Amber cleaned up the floor while Sandra wiped the stove. The ceiling would have to stay spotted for now.

"Bring your plates over," Sandra said. She offered a tired smile. "Let's get some warm food in you."

Beetle brought his right away, although Amber could tell he was still annoyed about being called Bernard.

Amber wanted to see what was on the tablet so she stepped to the side as Sandra scooped sauce onto Beetle's plate, burying (and perhaps warming) the string beans and pasta.

On the screen, there appeared to be a list of scores.

Punctuality: 85%
Preparation: 61%
Manners: 42%
Discourse: 50%

There were a few other things listed but Sandra grabbed the tablet before Amber could read them.

"Don't worry. We'll do better tomorrow."

Amber had so many questions. She wanted Sandra to explain where they were and how they got here, and she didn't care how many fairies or wizards or witches her mother included in her explanation. She wanted to share how things had been the past two days. How the other mother had cut her hair, and what had happened at the Parallels' building (although she'd probably leave out the chicken dinner since that might be especially upsetting). Yet she still felt under the gaze of that egg-shaped lens and just said, "Thank you," as her mother spooned the sauce onto her plate.

They sat back down, but Amber wasn't hungry. Beetle cleared his plate and asked for seconds, and Sandra waved him in the direction of the pot in a careless sort of way. She was looking out the darkened window, lost in thought.

Amber had expected that once they found their *real* mother everything would be okay, but instead everything was growing more and more strange. She felt as if she'd been trapped in a maze, like that time Sandra took them to a carnival and Amber got lost in the fun house. One of the employees, a teenager with a purple mohawk, had rescued Amber from the room of mirrors after identifying the correct version from the rows of crying girls in matching cutoff shorts.

Ten minutes later, another ding and the light on the egg camera changed from red to green. Their mother perked up. A fake smile slipped back in place. "Who's ready for dessert?"

Amber laid her napkin over her uneaten food. She had a feeling that there'd be a score issued somewhere for food waste or incomplete consumption. "I'll clear," Amber said.

She grabbed Beetle's plate as he shoveled a final noodle into his mouth. Her mother had taken only a small portion, and much of that was matted down as if to compost it on the plate.

"Thank you, Amber."

Sandra went to the counter and removed a pound cake from a grocery bag. Looking over her shoulder, she ripped off the plastic wrap, slipped the cake onto a plate, and shoved the wrapper into a drawer.

Beetle ate a slice in two bites and reached for a second piece.

Their mother addressed the camera as she said, "Slow down, dear. Our meals are meant to be enjoyed."

Sandra sounded as if she were reading from a guidebook. But Amber noted an edge, an edge she knew well enough to identify as sarcasm. Her mother turned to look at the opposite wall. There was a round clock that Amber had also missed earlier. It was white like the egg. As the hands moved to seven p.m. another dinger sounded, and as if on cue, Sandra announced, "Time for homework."

The eye camera closed once more.

Amber walked to the front of the apartment where she usually dropped her backpack. It wasn't there. Looking up, she spotted another egg camera over the door. She watched it as she backed down the hall to her bedroom. It stayed shut, the red light steady. She entered her room, but again, something didn't ring true. A vibe, her mother might call it.

The usual furniture was there: bed, desk, dresser, plus, in the spot that usually contained stacks of books, the bonus of a beanbag chair, something Amber had been requesting for what seemed like forever. There was also a bulletin board, like the one in her other room where she pinned photos and reminder notes. Instead of taking things down, she pinned new things over them, so by the end of each school year the board had developed layers of paper, like sediment. As a way to close out the year, she would take down anything related to school, put it in the recycling bin, and shout, "Summer!"

This bulletin board had only one layer and it looked as if a ruler had been used to space each item evenly. She spotted some familiar items: reminder notes about library day and swimming, a fancy invitation to Clara's last birthday party, and a strip of pictures of her with Debbie and Clara like the one she had at home. Her real home, that is. The strip contained four square images of their grinning faces; the red lettering at the bottom proclaimed *Best Buds.* The photo booth had been part of one of their earliest outings after a softball game in which barely anyone on the other team made it to first, thanks in large part to Amber. "Come to the movies with us. It'll be a blast," Clara had said. Amber remembered how good it felt to be squeezed into that tight little photo booth in the theater lobby with the two most popular girls in her grade.

She studied the photos. Something seemed off. Her expression was different. The Amber in the photo wore the haughty, tight-lipped look she'd seen in the window before she'd crossed through. And she was in the middle. With the exception of the softball team photo for the yearbook, Amber had never ever been in the center of any photo with Clara and Debbie. On the strip in her real room, she'd been pushed just slightly out of frame, so in each image a part of her was cut off—the top of her head, the side of her face.

She turned to examine the desk. It was also much neater than the one at home. It contained the usual assortment of pens and notebooks but none of the goofy things she'd picked up over the years. And the top of the radiator was empty. That's where she displayed her softball trophies. Her backpack was leaning against the desk chair. It matched the one she usually carried, but like everything else here, it seemed in better shape.

She scanned the corners of the room. No egg cameras. That was a relief. But she still felt that prickly feeling of being watched. Like that time a spider landed on her arm and she still felt it crawling on her after she'd flicked it away. Her mother had laughed at her shriek. "Spiders are good luck, you know. You should make a wish."

Amber had another wish that she used to make silently (with or without a spider) when she got especially fed up with her mother. Or maybe it was more like a fantasy. A fantasy for a type of parenting police, who would arrive at the door looking like Debbie's and Clara's mothers, or the mothers in TV commercials.

"Now, Sandra," the parenting police would say, shaking their stylish heads in reproach. "You have violated numerous codes," and they'd run through the list that included leaving children unsupervised, making only pasta for dinner, and filling impressionable young minds with silliness. Then they'd write a ticket and order Amber's mother to shape up, "and while you're at it, buy that wonderful daughter of yours a beanbag chair."

In Amber's fantasy, though, there were no cameras, and her mother gave up all her delinquencies as if she'd been put in a trance by one of her own imaginary creations. Was this another case in which Amber had in some way gotten her wish?

A knock on the door. Amber jumped. Her mother wasn't the only one on edge.

"Who is it?"

She wanted the answer to be: "It's your real mother and I'm going to tell you how we're going to get back to where we belong." Instead, she heard Beetle's soft voice asking to come in.

"Go away, Little Bug," she said. She didn't have any answers. Having to tell him that would only make her feel worse. He came in anyway. He was carrying something that looked like a medal.

She didn't spot any books, so her hand reached for a pillow. She poised it to throw. He stayed by the door.

"Is it her?" he asked.

"I think so," Amber said. "What are you holding?"

Beetle seemed to take that as an invitation to enter. He brought the object over. It was a medal in the shape of a soccer ball with the words *All-Star Champion.* In their real home Beetle had never competed on an organized team, soccer or otherwise, although he liked to kick the ball around and would go to the park for pickup games when Sandra told him he needed to get out for some fresh air.

Amber handed back the medal and brought the pillow to her chest. The pillowcase emitted the fake floral smell of commercial detergent, a smell she'd mostly encountered at Debbie's and Clara's. Sandra insisted on using an unscented natural brand since it was better for the environment, and she only ever washed their sheets when she'd gathered enough extra quarters for the machines. But Amber didn't take the recently washed bedding as a sign that it *wasn't* her, since it seemed like Sandra had elected to follow a mysterious set of unspoken rules. Rules that involved curfews and filmed dinners, neatness, and, quite possibly, clean sheets.

"I need to talk to her, but not around the you know what." Amber winked a few times, her impersonation of the egg lens opening and closing.

Beetle shook his head. "Huh?"

"The cameras. Didn't you notice the one in the kitchen? There's one by the front door too. And maybe others." She scanned the ceiling again, just in case one would be revealed from this angle. "It seems to be checking on what we're doing. There were some numbers that seemed like ratings when Sandra checked the tablet."

"Why?" Beetle asked.

"I don't know, but I'll try to find out. In the meantime, just play it cool and do what you're told, starting with getting your homework done. I have a feeling we don't want to know what happens if we don't." She felt the prickling again, as if the walls might have eyes.

After Beetle left, Amber took the books out of her backpack and checked the assignment planner. The handwriting was painfully neat, much neater than Amber's. Amber's letters mushed against each other, and she was always smearing what she'd just written. She wondered if this other girl might be right-handed instead of left. If those kinds of variances were possible, then maybe this other Amber didn't even play softball. She looked in the planner to see if an after-school practice had been listed. Soccer maybe. Or track. But the lined sections for Monday through Friday included only class homework. The assignments themselves were simple, as if her other self was a year behind, and Amber was able to get through the homework quickly, even the math. Although there was no helping the handwriting.

Amber hoped Sandra would come in to check on her. She could ask for a story about the fairy godmother or the witch. That could be a way to let her mother know that it was them, the real Amber and Beetle.

She ran her hand through her ponytail and realized how much she missed the feeling of her mother's fingers combing through her hair, even though the last time her mother tried, Amber had pulled away. When she was little, she would sneak up on her mother like an explorer in the wild. Instead of capturing a wild animal, her goal was to pet her mother's hair without her mother noticing. If her mother was reading a particularly good part in her book, Amber could get away with it for several minutes before Sandra laughed and swatted Amber's hand away. "Careful, you might lose a finger in there."

Amber peeked in the closet and the drawers. Everything was so perfectly neat. She went to use the bathroom. The toilet-paper roll was on the holder instead of perched on top. A buzzer sounded. Sandra called for them to brush their teeth, which Amber didn't do (she didn't like the idea of using someone else's toothbrush, even if it was sort of her own). She went back to her room, again hoping her mother might come in to check on her. She looked around for a book to read. Still didn't spot one. But no matter. A few minutes later, another buzzer and the lights went out. At first, Amber thought it was a power outage. She felt her way over to her light switch and flipped it up. The room stayed dark. Peeking into the hall she saw that Beetle's light was out, but her mother's bedroom light was on and she could hear her down the hall in the kitchen rinsing dishes.

She looked at the alarm clock next to her bed. It read nine p.m.

Amber never went to bed before ten, but lying in bed she realized how tired she felt. As much as she wanted to work on a plan for the next day, the darkness rested like a blanket, and her eyelids closed as she drifted off to sleep.

10

Amber's alarm clock woke her at seven a.m. She forgot for a moment where she was—not the part about being in her bed, but rather where her bed was located. The smell of coffee was familiar (her mother claimed she couldn't string two words together without it) but there were also unfamiliar smells, which, after a few sniffs, Amber identified as eggs and toast. Her body felt as tired as if it were still the middle of the night even though the yellowish-gray light filtering through the curtains suggested it was, indeed, day.

She checked her watch. 6:12 p.m. Cheap watch that it was, the battery was probably running low. One of Amber's many plugs for why she needed a cell phone had been that it would help with punctuality. Sandra had "Mhmm'd," and, a week later, presented Amber with the watch. "It has screens for the date, an alarm, *and* a stopwatch," Sandra had proclaimed when Amber tried to object. Any other day Amber would have welcomed the opportunity to prove that a cheap plastic watch was clearly NOT as reliable as a rechargeable phone.

Amber got out of bed. Her clothes from yesterday, which she'd tossed on the floor, had been folded and placed on top of the radiator. And the schoolbooks she'd left scattered were stacked neatly next to her backpack. Her mother must have come in during the night and straightened. In a dresser drawer she located clean jeans and a T-shirt. At least they fit the same, although like everything else in the apartment, they seemed almost new. No frayed edges. No holes. Her mother had always shopped for their clothes at secondhand stores, and there'd been times Amber had had to wear clothing marked with the name of the previous owner. But here was some good news, the first since this whole thing had started.

Neatly folded in the drawer was the pink shirt with the heart she'd been missing for weeks. Out of habit, Amber mumbled, "Thank you, Witch." When she spoke, she thought she spotted a shift of light in the room. Just for a beat. Then a buzzer went off.

Her mother called, "Amber, come to breakfast!"

Beetle was already seated at the table.

Sandra placed a carton of juice in front of him. "Amber, hurry. It's not like you to be late." She sat down as well.

The dinger sounded. Amber slid into her seat just as the light on the egg turned green. The lens slid up.

On the table Amber spotted the scrambled eggs and toast, along with small containers of jelly and butter and a bowl of syrupy strawberries. The only time Amber had eaten a breakfast like this was when she'd slept over at Clara's house. At home they ate generic dry cereal with whatever nondairy milk was cheapest, and, in colder months, oatmeal. Where had her mother gotten the money for this kind of food?

"What are you looking forward to at school today?" Sandra asked. The fake smile again, like a mask pulled in place. Her hair was twisted into a tight braid and she wore a white shirt with a logo stitched on a pocket, the letters *PFA* in the outline of a heart.

With everything going on, Amber hadn't really given much thought to school. She didn't feel ready to deal with the Debbie and Clara drama but wasn't about to mention it. Not for the camera or to her mother.

"Putting my head down, working hard, and doing my best," Amber answered. It was what their gym teacher, Mr. P., was always saying they should do.

Beetle snickered and she gave him a kick under the table. He was going to be a black and blue Beetle if he didn't get his act together.

"I want to see the Parallels," Beetle said.

Sandra looked up. "What did you say?"

Amber glanced up at the still-open egg eye. She rushed to answer ahead of Beetle. "That's just a game the kids have been playing to see who can hang the longest on the monkey bars." Her explanation didn't make any sense, but she hoped the eye was satisfied. It closed and the red light came back on.

As they ate, Amber could see her mother studying them, as if trying to identify something out of place: a twitch, a scab, a stray hair. Another buzzer. Beetle shoveled in the last bite of toast as Sandra said, "Get your school things."

Amber brought her plate to the sink, grabbed her backpack, and went to the front door. She had to admit that it took her a lot less time to get out of the house without having to search for her shoes and gather up all her schoolwork. Even the drawer in the bathroom where she usually had to dig around for a ponytail holder was well organized. But as she listened to her mother bang around in her bedroom, she suspected that the organizational project had happened prior to the swap.

"Just looking for the house keys," Sandra called.

Amber would have laughed except the egg lens by the door was sliding open. Her breakfast formed a softball-sized lump in her stomach as she pictured a countdown clock appearing on the wall. What would happen if they were late?

She didn't want to find out. She dropped her backpack and sprinted into her mother's room. On hands and knees, she searched while her mother dug in her purse. Amber spotted the keys on the floor by the bed, grabbed them, and said, "Looks like the witch was at it again."

She noticed a brief brightening, like a light switch dimmer turned up, but she was more interested in the flash of recognition on her mother's face.

Sandra placed her hand on Amber's hair. "Ember?" she said.

Amber nodded and didn't pull away.

Her mother pulled her into a hug. "Oh, sweetie, I feel like I haven't seen you in so long."

"I have so many questions," Amber said, her face pressed into her mother's shirt. She had never been happier to hear Sandra say that ridiculous name.

"We'll have a few minutes to talk outside," Sandra said. "Don't bring anything up on the bus."

Before Amber could ask what bus, they heard another buzzer. Amber followed her mother, her *real* mother, to the front door. So many things Amber didn't understand, but there was one thing she was sure of, she would follow *this* mother anywhere.

11

Sandra led them down the block to a white sign with the letters *PF*. The ground was damp and the clouds looked ready to drop more rain. Another woman waited at the sign. As Amber approached she saw that it was a younger, single mother from the next building over, with whom Sandra chatted sometimes. She also wore a white shirt and had woven her braids into a thicker braid. Her two children chased each other around a spindly tree.

Sandra nodded at the other woman, but there was nothing of their familiar exchange of "All good?" and "Can't complain, you?"

"Peter, Jasmine, stop," the woman ordered.

The children froze.

"Where's the car?" Amber asked. Beetle watched the kids compete in their statue contest. He'd burrowed one arm into his shirt and was trying to pull the other one in, which proved more challenging without a helper.

"Shh, not so loud."

Sandra looked around, although as far as Amber could tell, no egg-like orbs floated overhead. "They took it."

Amber tried to match her mother's volume. "Took it? Who? Why?"

"I was late getting you to school. But we can talk about that later. I want to know how you got here. Quick, there isn't much time."

Amber rushed through as many details as she could recall: the other mother's strange behavior, the cooking, and the haircut. "You were early *all* the time," she said with a smirk she couldn't restrain. She told about walking to the School Towel Service building at Magic Hour and that it let them pass through.

"One of the things I don't understand is how did the other me leave? The one who was here before; the one I saw on the other side of the glass."

"You swapped places," Sandra answered. "I still don't understand how it all works, but I imagine there can never be duplicates. One needs to be here, one there, although this wasn't a random occurrence. They must have seen it as an escape." She sighed. "I don't blame them."

Amber didn't like the idea of someone else, even another version of herself, sleeping in her bed and touching her things (but maybe that Amber would also avoid the toothbrush). Hopefully the other her turned out to be a decent athlete and wouldn't draw attention to herself or get into trouble. Also, what about Amber's actual school assignments? She had an English test coming up. She usually got As in English. Then again, maybe the homework she'd done last night was just a review.

Sandra looked down the street. "Here's the bus. We'll talk more tonight."

She gave Amber's shoulder a squeeze that was intended, Amber assumed, to feel comforting. But her mother's expression was anything but, and her grasp felt more like a grip.

The bus pulled to the curb, puffing gray exhaust. It was the size of a city bus, but painted white and had Protecting Families written in red across the side. The door whooshed open.

Sandra pulled Beetle's arm out of his shirt. "Whatever you do, just try to follow along today. Don't rock the cradle."

Amber couldn't help but smile. "The boat, Sandra. It's don't rock the boat."

On the bus, Sandra flashed a card at the driver, a thick-bellied woman, who nodded them on. There were a few other passengers already seated. They seemed to be women in white shirts with children. Many of the kids looked to be around Amber's and Beetle's ages, along with some little kids and teenagers. Amber spotted one pregnant woman sitting alone, staring out the window with a dull expression.

Amber had assumed this was a school bus and wondered why the women of the older kids were traveling to school with them. She got her answer when the bus stopped near the business section of town. The doors opened. The mothers said goodbye to their kids, stood, and streamed off, the pregnant woman among them.

"Have a good day at school," Sandra said, again with that forced brightness. She leaned over to kiss them. To Amber she whispered, "Go to the bus stop after school. I'll get back on here. Watch out for Beetle. Keep your head down. Everything will be fine."

Amber didn't feel like everything would be fine and she could tell that Beetle didn't either. He closed his eyes as if he were trying to pinch back tears.

"It's okay, Little Bug," Amber said, and gave him a friendly jab in the arm. "At least we don't have to deal with her driving."

He smiled but it looked as forced as Sandra's. For once Amber was glad that he didn't say much. Hopefully that would help him today. As the bus pulled away, Amber tried to keep sight of her mother but lost her in the crowd of white shirts and braids.

At least Amber knew where they were headed; her assignment planner had The Hastings School printed on the cover. Beetle didn't get his wish to see the Parallels that morning because they'd sat on the wrong side of the bus. Although Amber tried to see out the other side, she was only able to glimpse the rooftop of the School Towel Service building. She wondered if the Parallels were passing by at the same time. If so, would they see the bus? Amber imagined the other Amber's haughty look, the other mother relieved to have her actual children back, the ones with neat handwriting and good table manners and clean rooms.

The bus made a stop at the public middle school and one of the elementary schools, and finally pulled into The Hastings School parking lot. Amber and Beetle got off and joined the throng of kids who'd arrived by car. Now Amber wasn't envious just of the fancier cars, but of the fact that those families still owned one. She had so many questions to ask her mother, but first they had to get through the school day.

Their gym teacher stood at the school entrance. He wore a shirt like Sandra's but in navy instead of white, with matching navy pants.

"Hi, Mr. P.," Amber said.

"Keep walking," he said without offering his usual friendly high five.

Amber squeezed Beetle's shoulder, and he let her. She hoped it was gentler than her mother's had been. Beetle headed in the direction of the fourth-grade classroom while Amber made her way upstairs. It seemed like the typical morning bustle. Sneakers squeaked on floors that smelled of bleach and old mops. Lockers opened and shut with a slam. Kids shouted to each other down the hall. Something seemed off, but when Amber considered her surroundings she couldn't pinpoint anything unfamiliar. Perhaps she was still getting used to the odd light and slanted floor, although both were less noticeable today.

As she reached her own locker, Clara and Debbie rushed over.

"Amber, you missed it. Debbie just tripped Stuart Matthews and he totally wiped out."

"Yeah, it was awesome," Debbie said. "But it still doesn't beat what you did yesterday, Amber. Classic humiliation."

What had the other Amber done?

A buzzer sounded. Amber automatically glanced at the ceiling but didn't spot any cameras. She realized that it was just the first period bell.

"See ya later," Debbie and Clara said as they headed down the hall.

So, clearly the friendship issue wasn't something she'd have to deal with today. A relief, she had to admit, to be accepted again.

Amber checked the schedule taped to her locker and was grateful that her day's classes were the same, along with the classroom locations. But the classes themselves were another story. Or more like a joke with no punch line.

For one thing, she had different teachers. In English, a female teacher launched into a speech about banned books, but not in the way her usual English teacher, Mr. Brighton, would. (His declaration: "Books open the closed mind.") She nicknamed this teacher Ms. Pursed Lips since it would have been strange at this point in the year to ask the teacher for her name. Ms. Pursed Lips projected the covers of several books that Amber had read and loved (some in school, some out) and rattled off nonsense about needing to protect impressionable minds from "morally reprehensible" material. When she spoke she slapped the top of her desk as if it were one of the insolent book covers.

"Class, your homework tonight is to write an essay that includes three examples of what is considered reprehensible behavior at school."

Amber waited for everyone to laugh. No one did.

A similar thing happened in science class. She hadn't had science homework the night before so she wasn't sure what they were studying, but at her other school they'd been learning about evolution. If Amber had to rate her favorite classes, science was a close second to English, and it would have won out except for its dreaded math component.

She especially loved her science teacher, Ms. Stein, whose wild hair could rival her mother's, although Ms. Stein's was bright red. Ms. Stein had told them that as a child she'd begged her parents to change her middle name from "Lynne" to

"Eine" so she could be called "Eine Stein." Her parents said no, so instead she told everyone that her middle name was pronounced "Line" and therefore almost got her way.

"When you hit a wall, back up and find another way. There's *always* another way," Ms. Stein told them.

Amber even liked doing the science homework. She'd been midway through a paper on Darwinism, and sometimes she would keep reading the research after her homework was done because she found it all so interesting—that creatures crawled from the muck to breathe air, grew into apes and Neanderthals and the modern-day human, who was still, as the research noted, continuing to evolve. Wasn't it exciting, Amber thought, to wonder what would come next? Maybe they'd go back to being able to breathe underwater. Maybe they'd be able to fly.

This science teacher marched in front of the class as if he were leading a military drill. Spit flew when he spoke and Amber was glad she sat in the back row. She was seated between Debbie and Clara, who weren't in her other science class. But if they had been, she never would have gotten the coveted middle seat.

"Who will start us off with the recitation on the origin of man. Kevin?"

A boy in the second row stood. "Man was created in the image of the divine."

Ever since her English class, Amber had carried a pitted feeling in her stomach, as if all those flying insects from earlier had drilled holes in her belly and filled them with cement. Now the cement was hardening. She squinted at the boy. He looked like Kevin James from her school, but that Kevin had been suspended for two days for writing curse words (real ones, not her mother's) on the bathroom stalls.

"Yes, very good. Who wants to go next?"

During class Amber did not take a single note. How could she? She kept waiting for someone to shout in protest.

There'd never been anything related to religion in school before. The teacher must have noticed her perplexed expression.

"Amber, do you have a question?"

She blurted out, "Aren't there alternate theories?"

The room fell silent. Amber felt her cheeks turn red.

"Well, yes. What about them?"

"Well, I was just wondering if we'd be talking about them."

There were a few snickers, but a look from Mr. Military silenced them.

He marched over to a sign on the wall that Amber hadn't noticed. It looked like a list with very small words. The heading, however, appeared in large blocky red characters:

In Protection of Families

"It appears I need to remind you, as per state law, only creationism can be taught at the middle-school level. You will be able to refute other theories in high school. Perhaps you need to stay after class to review."

"Oh, that's right." Amber sank into her seat. "I just forgot."

"Way to go, Amber," Debbie said admiringly as they walked out of class.

"Yeah," said Clara. "You're such a rebel. You're lucky you didn't get sent to the *pen*."

Both girls shuddered.

Whatever happened, Amber told herself, she was not going to open her mouth in class again. If for no other reason than the pen did *not* sound like something she wanted to experience. But she wouldn't have minded taking a closer look at that sign. She spotted it on the wall of her next class too—dreaded math—but the teacher was a substitute, and they spent the class doing worksheets on division that Amber thought she might have done in fifth grade.

Lunch was a breeze. She had her old seat, and everyone

seemed to want her opinion. She'd been a little disappointed when she opened her backpack and saw a plain blue lunch sack (perhaps they didn't have Bionic Woman here?) but was considerably cheered by its contents: cheese sandwich, apple, and carrots.

After lunch they had recess.

"Headed to the field?" Debbie asked.

The three of them used to practice softball during recess. It was nice to have something that resembled normality, but Amber replied, "I need to catch up on homework. Looks like it's the library for me."

After the two girls ran off, Amber walked into the library and over to the row of desktop computers available for student use. She didn't see any other students, and the librarian was probably at lunch. While the monitor warmed up, she looked around. Many of the shelves were empty, as if all the books had been checked out. The search screen appeared. She entered Protection of Families. The top two links were for Wikipedia pages, one for Protection of Families Act and the next, Protection of Families Agency. She clicked the first one.

> The Protection of Families Act was created by a consortium of governors in thirty-six states to provide greater regulatory oversight for the care of minors. As noted by Governor Ron G. Vernon, who spearheaded the effort, "Our goal is nothing less than to put children first by ensuring that moral and ethical standards are achieved at both home and school."

A photo labeled Governor Vernon and his Cabinet showed a tan white man with unnaturally dark hair, surrounded by a group of other men. He might have been a candidate from one of their elections back home, but Amber couldn't remember.

She clicked the next link, which identified the Protection of Families Agency (PFA) as the state-run organization responsible for enforcing the Protection of Families Act.

Under a heading for Notable PFA Accomplishments, she read:

> Job placement service guarantees mothers of school-age children employment at the PFA or its partners (see PFA Sponsored Industries).
>
> Greatly reduces childhood hunger through distribution of food vouchers to families in need.
>
> Provides free housing options for homeless mothers with children (see PFA Family Farms).
>
> Ensures that all minors have equitable access to quality education through state-mandated curriculum.

These seemed like good things, but Amber could hear Sandra's voice in her head asking, "How many books?" (This was in reference to the time Amber signed up for a Book-of-the-Month Club that promised *Free Book Each Month!* Amber had missed the part about having to pay for three other books that arrived with it. An expensive mistake!) She scrolled down to a section labeled PFA Requirements for Services. The list included obvious things like giving kids nutritious meals and getting them to school and to bed on time. But one item gave her pause.

> Mothers who choose to raise children in single-parent homes are subject to more rigorous oversight through daily compliance checks. Those who fail to satisfy the necessary conditions can be subject to fines, terminated from PFA positions, and evicted from their homes. (Single fathers are exempt provided children are in school or under female supervision during working hours.)

At the bottom Amber spotted a thumbnail for the sign hanging in the classrooms. She clicked, made it full-screen, and located the clause against teaching evolution since it *violated the student's right to religious freedom.* That made it seem as if only one religion counted.

Out of curiosity she typed in Darwin, feeling like the rebel

Clara had claimed her to be. Most of the links were inactive. She turned to Wikipedia again:

> Darwinism, created by Charles Darwin (1809-1882) was a pseudoscience claiming man evolved from sea creatures.

What was going on? Darwin, a pseudoscientist? A law that discriminated against single mothers? It was like being in another universe.

Oh, wait. She was.

12

After school, Amber and Beetle lined up with the other kids at the bus stop. Beetle's shirt looked as if he'd been assigned the job of rope in a game of tug of war. She asked if he was okay. He nodded and gave a weak smile. She hadn't paid attention to the kids on the bus ride to school but now, in line, she spotted a few familiar faces, including Stuart Matthews.

Stuart was tall and scrawny, not one of the more athletic boys who had been part of her earlier friend group, although she remembered how, on that day in her other school, he'd offered to help remove the tape from her locker lock. When she smiled at him now, he looked down at his feet.

The carpool line thinned. Where was the bus? She was eager to get home and relieved that she had (mostly) made it through the day without drawing attention. Thankfully she hadn't been called on in her afternoon classes, but one thing she knew with certainty was that she hated being here. Even her newfound popularity wasn't that great. Her friends' favorite expression seemed to be "that's dumb." In fact, that seemed to be the favorite expression of everyone that day, and it had been offered up freely, along with "you're stupid" and "get a brain." When did everyone get so rude? It was just another reminder that this wasn't where she belonged. But how would they get back? Obviously it wasn't just a matter of walking by the School Towel Service building. Sandra would have gone back already if that were the case. What if they got stuck here? No, Amber reassured herself. Their mother would explain everything. She would get them home.

The bus finally pulled into the lot. Amber and Beetle followed the others on board.

This time Beetle selected seats on the opposite side of the bus, but they both failed to consider they'd be headed in the other direction. The bus stopped downtown and the mothers got on. Amber felt her pulse quicken—that nervous feeling she remembered from those endless waits in the pickup line—until she saw Sandra enter the bus and flash her card to the driver. Her mother looked tired. Loose hairs sprang from her braid. She made her way toward them.

"Everything okay?" Sandra asked, eyeing Beetle's shirt.

Amber nodded. As the bus started, Amber opened her mouth to speak, but Sandra put her finger to her lips. "We'll talk later."

Not speaking felt like forcing back a sneeze or a dry, raging cough. Amber just wanted to talk and talk and talk. She pressed her lips together and swallowed hard and was offered a distraction when video screens opened in the backs of the seats. A recorded voice announced, "Please take a moment to watch a complimentary video from Protecting Families."

Beetle had been leaning against the window with his head tucked in his shirt. His hair poked through the stretched-out neck. At the sound of the video, the tufts of hair rose, like a creature emerging from the Sea of Cotton.

Soft music played what Sandra would call elevator music, and a man's face appeared on the screen. He had short gray hair and watery blue eyes and looked like a newscaster.

"Hello. I'm Gary Graham, the CEO of the Protecting Families Foundation. We have been working alongside your elected representatives to ensure that every child has an equal opportunity to thrive. We know the challenges facing single mothers today and that is why we have created the Family Farms to guarantee that all children have a roof over their heads and good, plentiful food."

As he spoke, a montage of images showed a farm that looked as if it could be found in any Midwest town: cows chewing cud, chickens pecking at feed. Two smiling children dressed in overalls pulled vegetables in a garden and handed them to a woman, presumably their mother, who gave a wide smile. Another image showed a long table where women and children ate family style, serving themselves from steaming bowls of mashed potatoes and corn.

The children seated across from Amber watched the video with their fingers gripping their seats, as if to restrain themselves from grabbing for the food. They had bony knees and thin faces. Maybe they didn't qualify for the food vouchers that Amber had read about.

The video image cut back to the man as he walked around a corral where children rode horses. Amber thought he looked funny with riding boots over his fancy suit pants, as if he'd made a mistake getting dressed that morning and grabbed the wrong shoes. Although there was something about him that made it seem like he never made mistakes.

"Here at the Family Farms, we put families first each and every day. Come see what we have to offer." The camera zoomed in. The man smiled. He had a grandfatherly type of smile.

The screen flashed a website and phone number.

One of the children in the other row tugged her mother's sleeve. "Can we go? Can we? Please, please?"

It made Amber think of a kid clamoring for a visit to a water park. True, the farm looked nice, but if her mother had taught her anything it was don't believe it until you see it with your own eyes. Sometimes a witch lurked. Sometimes fairies dressed branches with dew. And sometimes people on TV told lies. Take, for instance, the Unbreakable Bubble Ball.

The Unbreakable Bubble Ball was a giant inflatable plastic bubble that supposedly never popped. Amber had begged Sandra to get it for the holidays after seeing it advertised on a show she'd watched at Debbie's house. On principle their mother was against "the capitalistic pressure to provide unnecessary gifts to whiny children," but nevertheless, small items would appear for Amber and Beetle on or about the time other children in other households received gifts. As for the Unbreakable Bubble Ball, although Sandra proclaimed the item to be too good to be true, she gave in. Likely because it was cheaper than any of the other items on Amber's wish list, which included a cell phone in three places. The Unbreakable Bubble Ball popped the first day. Sandra stuck the deflated ball in a bowl on the kitchen counter to remind Amber and Beetle that advertising claims were a "crock of nonsense."

The bus turned onto their block and screeched to a stop. Amber was glad to be free of it. The sky still had the same off-putting color, as if someone had covered it with a mustardy-yellow scarf but at least it wasn't raining.

As they walked toward the building Sandra said, "We'll have an hour to ourselves after check-in. What do you say we go for a walk-it?"

"That's great!" Amber said.

Beetle nodded and extracted an arm from his shirt to offer a thumbs-up.

Inside, Sandra went straight for the tablet. Amber followed, and again she tried to see what was on it but was blocked by her mother's back. The egg camera had opened and was watching them through its glassy eye. Amber imagined a row of chickens on the other side, squawking at what they saw. It was a funny picture and she smiled, wanting to share it with her mother. Maybe that would take the slump out of her shoulders.

Sandra sighed. "Wash up. Grab a snack." Then, turning to the camera, she added, "Please make it a healthy choice."

Amber found an apple, a box of crackers, and half a bag of mini carrots that looked several days past expiration. Clearly her mother was overdue for a shopping trip. Perhaps this was Amber's chance to make a few recommendations. Her mother was always telling them to "make the best of things," and chocolate chip cookies sure would help. She took the bag of snacks to the front door. Beetle met her there with a soccer ball.

Although Beetle wasn't naturally athletic, he'd always been welcomed into the pickup games in the park. These games met Sandra's two requirements for extracurricular activities: fun and free. And Beetle did have fun, even if he sometimes tripped over the ball or sent it down the wrong side of the field.

Sandra joined them at the door. She'd changed into a button-down, likely the one she'd been wearing the day before. Amber spotted a tell-tale tomato sauce stain on the sleeve.

"Sorry, Beetle. You're only allowed to play soccer on Tuesdays and Fridays."

More rules! How did their mother, who couldn't keep days of the week straight, manage to stay on top of all of them? Amber's stomach gripped. She waited until the egg eye had shut, then asked, "Sandra, exactly how long have you been here?"

"I haven't been keeping very good track. What do you think, about two weeks?"

"You've been gone two days!" Amber said.

"Two days, really?"

Sandra looked as though Amber had just told her the earth was flat (although given that earlier science lesson, perhaps that was part of state law too).

Was it possible their mother had disappeared well before they'd noticed? Amber tried to pull up memories leading to that Wednesday morning in the car, but as anyone who has tried this can attest, it's nearly impossible to recreate a mundane day beat for beat. Surely Amber had eaten pasta every night for dinner and had cheese sandwiches every day for lunch. Maybe meals could be faked, but not the witch stuff. That had definitely been their actual mother losing her key and spilling coffee and making them late to school.

"Tell us what happened," Amber said. "Everything you remember. Why and how and especially what we can do to get home."

Sandra looked at the egg. It had closed but she shook her head and put her hand on Amber's shoulder. "Instead of a walk-it, let's find a place where we can sit and chat."

At the park, they chose a spot away from the afternoon activity. As Sandra had noted, only baseball was being played. In their real park different types of games were always going on—soccer and baseball and maybe some form of tag. The ball from a soccer game might land in the baseball diamond so a baseball player would kick it out of the way, and the baseball player might decide they'd rather be playing soccer. Or a soccer player would scoop up a baseball and give it a toss. Amber always joined the baseball games. When it was her turn to pitch, she would throw overhand, teasing, "You boys aren't strong enough for my fast pitch." The boys might tease back about her running like a girl, which they likely wished they could do, given all the bases Amber had stolen over the years. There were never any adults around to encourage "nice talk" or to help with team selection, but somehow the kids always worked it out. And they did it without calling each other "dumb" or "stupid."

Now, stern-looking adults in baseball caps appeared to be squarely in charge. Amber thought it looked like practice for a high-stakes travel team, the kind Clara and Debbie were talking about joining next year for softball. (Amber had known better than to ask her mother about trying out. Even if she could get a scholarship to cover the fees, her mother would never be able to drive her to all the games.)

The players, all boys, looked like mini clones of each other. In one area, boys practiced fielding; in another, they practiced batting; and off home plate, they were busy pitching and catching. The coaches circled the perimeter and barked orders or blew whistles. A few girls, siblings perhaps, watched from the sidelines or looked at their phones.

"When do the girls play?" Amber asked.

"They don't," Sandra said, spreading a blanket.

"You mean they don't play in this park?" Amber looked around. Even with all the stations there was plenty of empty park space farther down, although it appeared a bit muddy.

"No, I mean, girls don't play sports," Sandra said as she settled onto the blanket and crossed her legs. "It appears that organized sports for women don't exist here. Perhaps they never had Title IX or somehow managed to regulate it away. You do know what Title IX is?"

"Something to do with colleges, right?" Amber sat and also crossed her legs. Beetle copied, as if they were setting up for circle time at summer camp.

Another sigh from Sandra. "Do you *ever* listen to my talks? Yes, Title IX addresses gender discrimination by requiring schools to provide equal opportunities and funding regardless of sex. When it was passed in the 1970s, it really expanded women's athletics, not just at colleges but from high school on up to professional teams. I suppose, without these later opportunities, girls here lack role models, and there's no encouragement or motivation to play just for fun. Plus, girls aren't allowed to play on boys' teams. Apparently it's too dangerous." Sandra let out a snort. This time there was no mistaking the sarcasm.

No sports! Amber looked over at the boys playing. She tried to imagine what it would be like to have showed up at her own park and have Hector or Lewis tell her she wasn't allowed to play. She would have just picked up a ball and said, *I'm in whether you want me or not, and you better run fast to first.* She couldn't imagine going through school without the softball team. Such a big part of herself would have been missing.

"Boys rule, girls drool," Beetle offered.

Amber glared at him. "What do girls do all day? Just sit around and paint their nails?"

"Oh, girls are working on something, I imagine," Sandra said. "Working toward their MRS degree." She made a lemon-pucker face.

Amber made one too. "Well, what about women who don't want to marry men? Or women who just want to stay single?"

"That all falls under PFA regulations, I suppose. I've been trying to read the full law, but it's quite dense. Now, tell me about your school day."

Beetle picked up the apple. "It was weird." He took a bite, a sure way to stop further questions.

Amber filled her mother in on what had happened with the teachers and lessons (although she kept her friends' rude behavior to herself), and what she'd found at the library. "The article made the PFA sound like it was doing good work."

Sandra snorted. "It's a social net that's meant to ensnare. They've sold it as a way to support what they're calling non-traditional families, but really it's a cover-up for gender discrimination."

Amber sensed her mother might launch into lecture mode. "We want to hear about how you got here. Tell us everything you remember, in order."

Amber thought it best to approach information chronologically, the way backtracking helped when they were searching for Sandra's keys. She wished she'd thought to bring a notepad and pen.

Sandra got one of her faraway looks, as if she were trying to remember where she'd set down her book. "Well, let's see, it was on that day we were running late for school."

Amber smirked. "We're always running late."

Sandra smiled and reached over to tap Amber's shoe. "Yes, but you were particularly mad at me that morning."

Amber felt as if she might burst into tears. What if this did turn out to be her fault? She'd stepped on the crack with a bad wish that she hadn't even meant.

Sandra noticed her expression. "No, no. You didn't have anything to do with it. I know this will sound crazy—"

If Amber's mother was saying it would sound crazy, then it really must be a bonkers idea, but anything other than it being Amber's fault was just fine.

"See, I think the Parallels planned it. We'd been inviting them to visit for all these years. As this world started to go downhill, they took us up on our offer."

"But how did they know it would be better? I mean couldn't it have been the same, or even worse?"

"I think they assumed it wasn't worse because they saw us each day in the window. But that could be why the mother came first. To scope things out. She must have assumed I'd be a suitable enough temporary replacement, and, I suppose, to make sure that crossing over was safe. It was certainly unpleasant. We'd just stopped at the red light by the School Towel Service. I saw my reflection and said hello to my Parallel and that's when I assume it happened. I felt as if I'd been pulled underwater and couldn't catch my breath. That feeling passed by the time the light changed, but it took me until I got back to the apartment before I'd figured out that I had become the strange object in a new land, and everything hadn't just gone all Mercury in Retrograde. My Parallel was kind enough to leave me quite a thorough instruction manual that lists the rules and the schedule and where I should report to work, that sort of thing. I think she wanted to make sure I didn't alert suspicion while her kids were still here. Of course, that happened anyway with the car."

A rabbit hopped from a bush and nibbled at the dead grass. Sandra tossed a shriveled carrot its way.

"I must be fooling the cameras well enough since the food vouchers are still arriving. Although there wasn't much to choose from at the grocery store this week. Thank goodness pasta stays well stocked. But there's only limited fresh produce, and nothing that's been imported. Well, except for us." Sandra offered a wry smile.

Amber had so many important questions to ask, but selfish curiosity won out. "What was I like?" she asked, thinking of the haughty look when she met her Parallel face to face (well, face to glass to face).

"A tween," Sandra said with a shrug. "Before I realized I'd changed places, I worried you were becoming a mean girl. I remember thinking, *Oh no, not my Ember.* But then I realized it was just a young girl's defense mechanism. And Beetle, you were rather brusque."

Amber looked at the field so her mother couldn't see her face. Had she been on her way to becoming that girl by being friends with Clara and Debbie? Perhaps she should be grateful that they'd turned on her, although that other Amber, the one with the look, might have won them back. She worried about kids like Sarika. She hadn't noticed Sarika at school today, but there'd been a lot to take in.

The first batter struck out and started crying. One of the coaches yelled and made the kid stand against the fence. Amber wondered why the coach thought this would help with either the crying or getting the kid to base faster. She couldn't imagine her own coaches ever yelling like that, although Coach Dee did get a bit red in the face when they fumbled an easy play.

Sandra gestured at the field. "As you can see, there's a lot less civility here in general. But everyone, even the families who aren't as directly impacted, is acting out of fear. It's hard to be on your best behavior when you're always being watched."

"You mean by those egg things?"

"Well, yes, that's part of it, and I think that might have been the last straw for the other me, but it's not like the idea is so far out of the realm of normal. There's plenty of surveillance in our world too."

Sandra pointed to the security camera on the nearest light pole. Amber was relieved to see it pointed toward the players.

"Those are everywhere at home. And think about cell phones. Why do you think I don't want you to get one yet? I don't want all of your actions tracked, stored, and sold." Sandra pulled a stick out of Beetle's hands after he swatted two clumps of dirt into her lap. "Plus, they really limit imagination. What happened to spending time staring at the clouds, or looking at scenery? Now it's just eyes on a little screen."

"Sandra, you're getting off topic."

Her mother shrugged. "So the egg cameras—they're called Maternal Monitors, if you can believe it—are voluntary. Traditional households can elect to self-report and use a phone camera for scheduled check-ins. But for households that don't meet the threshold, the Maternal Monitors are much better than the alternative, which are unscheduled site visits. At the PFA I've heard rumors of vans coming in the night to cart off single mothers and their kids to the Farm. An *egg-xaggeration*, I'm sure."

Beetle laughed. Amber rolled her eyes.

"At least with the cameras there's some sort of record. Some burden of proof that you're not up to par."

"The Farm is that place we saw on the bus," Beetle interjected. "It seemed nice."

"Unbreakable Ball," Sandra said. "It's all in the marketing."

"How do you know?" Amber asked.

"At the PFA we get rotated through departments. After I lost the car, I was demoted from Administrative Support to Communications. This week I've been reviewing emails and posts from Farm residents to make sure everything is *PFA friendly*."

Their mother smiled the smile she used for the cameras.

"Sounds like they might be having some issues with overcrowding. And I've read several complaints about the work requirement for the kids. I'm guessing they're using the mothers and kids to fill the gap from all the migrant workers who got deported. We're supposed to notate any complaints so the PFA can address the needs of the Farm residents. But I suspect they're trying to keep track of bad publicity."

"Isn't it illegal to read people's mail?" Amber thought this was the case, although she couldn't remember the reason. Her social studies class wouldn't be starting the unit on the Constitution for two more weeks. Would she be there for it? She swatted the idea away like it was a bug, then remembered the part in the article about thirty-six states with similar laws.

"Well, why don't people move to a state that doesn't have these laws? Or aren't there still fifty?"

"I wondered that too. Apparently, you'd need something called an OSTA card."

"A what?"

"Out-of-state travel authorization. They issue them to wealthy tourists and to businessmen who travel for work. Kind of like a domestic passport. But from what I gather, the states that haven't passed similar laws are struggling. The federal government cut funding and put limits on utilities, food, and even clean water. And there's no option to leave the country. The borders have been closed. Not that I expect any other countries would want us."

"Well, at least this isn't happening everywhere in the world, right?"

"Hard to say. The government has managed to close the internet borders, too, so there's no access to foreign news. But even back home many countries treat women, especially unmarried ones, like secondhand citizens. Still, the changes here seem to be escalating at a rate that's faster than I could imagine."

Amber didn't think there was anything outside the

boundaries of Sandra's capacious imagination. She mouthed the word *capacious* because it reminded her of how happy she'd been when she'd gotten extra credit for using it in an English essay. Mr. Brighton wrote, *I appreciate your capacious vocabulary.* Was that really just last week? How she missed him, and Ms. "Line" Stein. She'd give anything for stacks of regular grumble-worthy homework. Even math.

A cheer from the field as a player rounded for home was soon matched by *boos* from the other side.

Sandra shook her head. "Do you know there aren't even any public libraries here? There were a few books in the apartment, thankfully. But I haven't seen a single person reading. How will they develop curiosity? Or empathy? I can't really speak to cause and effect. Just that there seems to be such an overwhelming amount of drivel. I mean, how many covers of "Stairway to Heaven" does one world need? Here, every TV show is a remake, although they've been cleaned up to reflect *modern values*." Another lemon-pucker face.

"We have a TV?" Amber asked. Maybe there was something to look forward to.

Sandra shook her head. "Just the monitoring tablet. One of the 'maternal requirements' is that we log a certain amount of news viewing each day. It's brainwashing is what it is. Hearing things repeated over and over. Opinion becomes fact. Belief becomes ideology. No questioning allowed. People here gobble up the news like it's an all-you-can-eat dessert buffet at Baker's Square. At first it was probably to stay informed. Maybe a little rubbernecking."

"What's that?" Beetle looked intrigued, likely thinking how much easier it would be to tuck a rubber neck into his shirt.

"It's when people slow down to stare at an accident," Amber said. Not that their mother ever slowed down for anything but a red light, and, even then, she'd missed a few.

"That's right," Sandra said. "Or seeing something bad

happening in someone else's yard, or natural disasters in another part of the world. People get hooked. It's really just another type of addiction."

Amber sensed Sandra was about to launch into a segment of "Advice from Your Mother."

"So do women even go to college here?" Amber asked. "Or have careers?"

"Well, college is very expensive; that's nothing new. And without merit aid or athletic scholarships, I imagine it's impossible for all but the rich. By the time girls your age are adults, I bet they won't realize that it could be normal to want a college education."

"So Clara and Debbie would be able to go, but not me?" Amber wanted to kick something. Instead, she picked up the stick and poked Beetle's leg.

"Ow." He scuttled out of reach.

"Oh, Ember." Sandra pulled the stick from her hand. "You know I'd work five jobs at a time if it meant giving you that opportunity. I've always felt that way. And as for careers, working women face the same challenges as they do in our world, just exponentially harder. Take childcare. Schools are actually banned from offering extended-care programs. But that's one way the PFA has made itself so appealing. They have a mandated nine a.m. to three p.m. workday for mothers. Although fathers can work until five-thirty to be home for dinner curfew. And women can advance within the Structure." Yet another pucker face, this time with an added *blech*. "That's what I call the building that houses the local PFA. I suppose working there is a privilege since lower-skilled women are assigned to factories and food service."

Amber had been pulling at the clumps of brown grass. She wondered why the grass was dead, given all the rain here. Everything seemed illogical. And so incredibly unfair. And her mother hadn't said anything yet about how they were going to get back.

Before she could ask, a boy yelled, "Heads up!"

A baseball sailed toward them. Amber jumped up and caught it barehanded. Shaking her hand, she pulled back and sent it soaring in the other direction. It was a perfectly aimed throw, but the boy didn't reach out to catch it. Amber saw the coach nearest him shake his head no.

"What is this?" Amber said. "They can't even catch a ball thrown by a girl?"

Sandra looked up at the security camera. "We'd better go."

As they walked back, a small circular craft appeared overhead.

"Squirrel UFO," Beetle declared.

Their mother used to tell them that if an alien life-form visited—and, as she pointed out, there was no reason to think it wouldn't—then it was just as likely to arrive in rodent form as any other.

Sandra shook her head as the small craft trailed them to the apartment. "That's a camera drone. Someone may have reported us."

"Reported us for what?"

"Who knows? Loitering. Or maybe a coach was mad that you have a stronger arm than any of those boys. Let's get inside, and we'll try to do well at dinner. I'm afraid it's pasta again, but if we put butter on and mush it into a ball shape, we'll get away with it. I'll call it smushed semolina or tortellini terrine. They don't have enough imagination to think it's anything other than what I enter on the website. One day, they'll put sensors in plates and then we're really done for."

She laughed but it wasn't a real laugh.

Amber didn't find it funny either. She had so many more questions to ask. A police car passed them and she tensed. She remembered how, back home, some of the kids she played with at the park would freeze when a cop car drove by. Amber used to think of the police as helpers, and that if you're not doing anything wrong, there was nothing to worry about; but now she better understood that maybe the thing you're doing is just being yourself. She realized it wasn't only Sarika who she hadn't seen at school that day.

"Sandra, is it just single women who are getting targeted or religions too?"

"Oh, yes." Sandra nodded. "I've been told there hasn't been a Muslim living in the area for at least two years."

As they reached the front of the apartment, the drone swooped past. The police car had pulled in behind a white van parked in front of the next building. The male officers got out. Two female guards in navy blue PFA uniforms left the building, followed by the neighbor from the bus stop. She carried a bag in each hand. Peter and Jasmine had backpacks and clutched stuffed animals. The policemen watched with bored expressions.

"What about all our things?" the woman protested.

An officer put up his hand. "Ma'am, I suggest you calm down. Since you've been unable to pay your fines, your personal property is now owned by the state."

"Where are we going?" Jasmine asked.

"You get to go to the Farm." The guard had the tone of a parent trying to make a visit to the dentist sound fun. "You'll like it there. Lots of animals and trees. And you'll all stay together. Isn't that what matters?" She patted Jasmine's head, as if patting one of the farm animals.

Amber couldn't hear if Jasmine answered because they'd climbed into the van. The door slid shut. One of the police officers met Amber's eye and she looked down. Why? She wasn't guilty of anything other than a regular curiosity. But what about the woman? What had she done, or not done? Amber felt her mother's arm on her shoulders, gently this time, guiding her toward the door. She didn't see the van pull away.

13

That night Amber and Beetle paid careful attention to the alerts and the egg camera as they set the table, ate their dinner (smushed semolina actually wasn't that bad), and worked on their homework. Yet again, Amber breezed through it. She was relieved that she didn't have to write any essays like "Kudos to Creationism" or "Yay, Banned Books." The English teacher's essay was easy, thanks to Amber's library research. But one big assignment remained. They needed to find a way to return to their world. And soon!

Amber picked up Lion—or, at least, the parallel version, who seemed equally willing to listen—and started to pace. But the more she paced, the more upset she became. She couldn't understand why her mother was playing by the rules. Why hadn't Sandra just walked up to that egg camera and shouted, "No more," then grabbed the other Amber and Beetle and run to the School Towel Service building? They could have fixed all these problems on their own side of the window, where people were still sane. Amber knew that didn't make sense. Sandra could have been lost to them forever if what she'd said was true about no duplicates. Amber fell back on the bed and hugged Lion to her chest. She was just a kid. How was she supposed to figure this out?

"Lion, I think this calls for a family meeting. Pronto."

Back when things were normal, at least as normal as they could be at home, they'd called family meetings for all sorts of reasons. To air grievances. Or because Sandra wanted to tell one of her stories. Or because everyone seemed low energy and a dance party might help. Amber's complaints were almost never resolved—demands for a cell phone and lunch variety, two recent examples—but it was nice to be allowed to parade in front of her mother and Beetle as if she were in charge.

Amber found Beetle in his room. He'd also finished his homework and was performing toe taps on a soccer ball with his head and arms buried in his shirt. She held back the urge to knock him over. "Family meeting," she said. "Sandra's room. Five minutes."

Sandra sat at the kitchen table, watching a video on her tablet. She shook her head and muttered, "That can't be." When she noticed Amber, she blacked out the screen.

"Sandra, I think we should have a family meeting. We need to get moving, right? Figure out how to get back."

Amber heard her voice crack, all the emotions vying to push through. She wanted to throw something at the egg camera and smash the tablet that was making her mother so upset.

Sandra nodded. Everything about her seemed limp—her hair, her expression, her hands as she set the tablet face down on the table, even her voice when she said, "Yes, that's a good idea." There was a look in her mother's eyes that Amber had never seen before. Amber couldn't remember the word to describe it. Something with a *D*. But whatever it was, it wasn't good.

It turned out there was a camera in Sandra's room too—"You forget about it after a while," she said with a shrug. "I just change in the bathroom."—so they ended up in Amber's room. Beetle, clearly relishing the continued access, grinned from the beanbag chair.

How could someone forget about being watched? Amber had not forgotten for one microsecond that cameras lurked in the corners. She felt as if they were part of some sick reality TV show. She thought about what Sandra had said earlier, how there were cameras back in their world too. And true, she rarely thought of them, even when she'd acted obnoxious with her friends at the mall, or let them film her for social media, sending all their photos into a virtual world. She never really thought about who might be in the audience.

Sandra slid to the floor. She leaned against the wall and hugged her knees to her chest.

Defeated. That was the word Amber had been searching for.

"So here's what I think," Amber said, as she started to pace again. "Tomorrow we need to go to the Parallels' building right at Magic Hour and try to get through. Let's kick those imposters back to their own screwed-up world."

Amber kicked over her trash can for emphasis. Crumpled papers spilled to the floor. She righted it but left the mess to clean up later.

Sandra sighed. "I wish it were that easy. First of all, if you haven't noticed, it's almost always overcast here, so it's hard to peg Magic Hour. And before I lost the car, I tried going by the School Towel Service building five or six times, but it was always just me in the reflection. I think there has to be a convergence in some way. Either both parties need to want to change or we have to have a similar enough schedule to cross paths. I'm guessing that's how the other mother made the swap, by seeing us and making a conscious choice to cross over. I thought I'd figured that option out. I kept ignoring the buzzer and was purposely leaving late, because I thought if I drove by at the same time you did, I could repeat the swap."

"That's dumb," Amber said.

Her mother gave her a sharp glance. "Listen here, young lady, I don't care what's going on. We don't talk to each other that way."

Amber blushed. "I'm sorry. What I meant was the other mother was always on time, so by you going late, you were already missing us. Plus, if it's really been two weeks since you got here, then the time wouldn't have matched anyway. You could have been driving by while we were eating dinner."

"Chicken," Beetle offered.

Amber knew he was identifying their meal and not offering a further insult.

Sandra tapped Amber's toe as Amber's pace put her in reach. "You've always had good deductive reasoning. You're right about the other mother's punctuality. But I didn't know then that she was all that different. Nice to know that I'm truly an original. But by then I'd decided to sit tight and follow the trash-can rule."

Every kid knew the trash-can rule—if you ever get lost, you stand at the nearest trash can since you have a better chance of being found if you stay in one place. (Beetle, over the years, had been located near several trash cans, and, a few times, inside them.)

"I felt you were safer back home, but I assumed the mother had a plan to get her kids to join her. If she managed the swap, I wanted to be here for you, and not have us all jumping back and forth like a game of parallel musical chairs."

"So you didn't have to lose the car after all." In their world Amber would have been thrilled to be free of that rattling, rusty embarrassment, but now it felt like losing their escape pod after crashing on a foreign planet. Although she suspected that was as farfetched as when she and Beetle used to think a cardboard appliance box could be transformed into a rocket ship.

Sandra worked a strand of her hair out of the braid. It sprang loose, like a prisoner freed from capture. "I probably would have lost the car anyway. I'm sure this won't surprise you, but I haven't had an easy time fitting in here, even with the mother's instructions. And being watched so closely seems to make me mess up even more. When they came to get the car, I couldn't find the key and they had to call a tow truck."

Amber had to smile. No surprise there.

"Let me tell you, they were not happy. But I've been giving this a lot of thought."

Now they were getting somewhere. "About getting home?"

"More about how life here became so restrictive. I think politicians had been laying the groundwork for years, if not decades, but it took that one big federal and state election for the more extreme policies to take root. Remember four years ago, when I said we'd dodged a disaster?"

Amber didn't, but she tended to tune out her mother's speeches, especially the ones that began with "every vote counts." Amber once told her she was pontificating, and Sandra's response was "five points for word choice, minus ten for attitude."

Sandra stretched out her legs and rubbed her knees. "Well, clearly they didn't dodge it here. It opened the door for establishing the PFA. But we still have enough in common for our two worlds to have touchpoints. I mean, there are plenty of similarities. We have state laws that are equally terrible, which hurt social services, immigrants, and education, and, yes, single mothers too. Again, in this world it's just taken to an extreme. And last fall's election went a different way for them too, making the crazier policies even easier to ramp up. Although I can't quite figure out to what end, outside of supporting a patriarchal system."

Amber renewed her pacing. What Sandra said made sense, and she tucked away the idea that things weren't all that rosy in her own world either. But it still didn't solve the problem of how to get back. Clearly it wasn't as easy as following the prompt to *walk through it.* She realized she hadn't told her mother about the strange notes in her lunch box or what had happened on the way home from school. She rushed through it now.

"I thought I saw you in the window of the School Towel Service building that last afternoon before we crossed over. But that couldn't have happened, right? Because of the time difference."

"Interesting." Sandra's fingers returned to her hair. "I wonder if that was another parallel world you were seeing?

Like a bridge between our world and this one. Or it could have been a vision of what you wanted to see, or time bending backwards in some way and you were seeing one of my earlier trips." She tugged at a snag in her hair and grimaced. "Time is, after all, merely a human construct. There's a lot to muddle over here." She untwisted the last part of the braid and gave her head a shake.

Amber longed to put her head on her mother's shoulder and tent herself under her mother's cascading hair. Instead she kicked Beetle's foot out of the way. He curled into a sort of nesting doll: a Beetle ball inside the larger ball of the chair.

"It's fascinating to think about," Sandra continued. "You mentioned looking up Darwin earlier. Well, think of our two worlds as emerging from the same common ancestor, but they began to evolve in different directions. I imagine the farther this world moves from resembling the one we left, the more they begin to misalign in other ways. Time is one example. We can look at it like train cars." Sandra put her hands next to each other to illustrate. "For a while our worlds were on parallel tracks but then they got routed to different destinations, and the tracks curved away from each other." She swerved her hands out. "The farther apart they travel, the more the view out of the window alters and weather patterns change. Ride long enough and you're in another time zone. It's likely that I contributed to that change when the other mother pulled me over, and that accelerated time by broadening the difference. Interesting, don't you think?"

Beetle nodded but Amber didn't find it interesting at all. She found it terrifying. "So how are we going to get back?"

Sandra got her pensive look again. "Well, the one thing we have on our side is that we don't belong. It's as if we boarded the wrong train and don't have a valid ticket. I have a feeling this universe recognizes us as alien. It wants the normal order to be restored."

Amber picked up a sheet of paper that had spilled from

the trash and crumpled it into a tighter ball. A "feeling" did not suggest strong scientific evidence, but it could be good news. *Evict us, strange, scary world*, Amber thought. *Throw us out on the street, just as long as that street has blue skies and it's not here.* She tossed the paper ball in the air. Caught it. Tossed again.

The ball-shaped Beetle in the chair piped up, "Like white blood cells."

"What?" Amber and Sandra asked at the same time.

He uncurled. "How white blood cells know when something invades your body, a virus or something, and then the cells turn into an immune army to kick the virus out." He kicked one foot, then the other to illustrate. "We learned about it last week at school."

Sandra sighed. "How I miss real science. You know the other day on one of the programs we have to watch there was this 'scientist' who claimed car exhaust actually helps the environment and discourages an overpopulation of birds. Anyway, yes, that's a great analogy, Beetle, but I think we'd only want that to happen if the trains veer back toward each other, as if they were meeting up at a shared station. If we can get to one of the stations, we can try to change to the correct train. We just need to figure out the touchpoint." She put the tips of her fingers together. "Make sense?"

Amber nodded. "But wouldn't one of the trains have to either slow down or speed up? Otherwise they'll never get there at the same time?"

"I don't know if that's how it works. Maybe one train takes a long way around so they still get there at the same time. Maybe it's not even a major touchpoint. Like you don't need to be in the same physical place. Maybe it's just someone here coming up with the same idea at the same time as someone there, while both are looking at a reflective surface, and it bends them toward each other."

"What about here at the apartment. Could that be a touchpoint?"

"I assume not, or else the other mother would have come that route. Plus, the only mirror is in the bathroom, and we're never in there at the same time."

Amber paced faster. The way Sandra described it made her think of two trapeze artists trying to switch trapezes in mid-air while swinging on opposite sides of a gym. At different times of day! If what her mother said was right, they could be getting even farther apart. Maybe it wasn't just two weeks but two months. Or two years! She felt ill, or maybe it was nerves. She stopped pacing and swung her arm back to pitch the paper ball. Her elbow knocked the lamp off the desk, which landed in the trash can.

"Two points," Beetle offered.

The buzzer went off. Sandra and Amber startled and Beetle rolled back into a ball.

"It must be close to bedtime," Sandra said. "I need to go check the monitor."

"What do you keep looking at?" Amber asked.

"I don't want you guys to get worried. Our numbers are a little low. I have to offer explanations for any rating below 75 percent. But tomorrow we'll hit every buzzer on the dot. They watch you at school too, so do your best."

"What happens if our numbers aren't good?" Amber asked.

"Don't worry," Sandra said, as she pushed to stand, but her expression suggested she wasn't taking her own advice.

Earlier, Amber couldn't think of a *D* word and now they flowed freely: *Depleted, Desperate, Distraught.*

"You said this universe doesn't want us." Amber heard her voice rise, out of her own sense of *desperation.* "So maybe we encourage it by making ourselves even more out of place."

Sandra shook her head. "No. For now you need to play along. Follow the rules. Okay?" She walked to the door.

Amber's voice jumped again. "We can't just sit around waiting. We have to *do* something!"

Sandra's tone was firm. "What *you* need to do is get ready for bed." She walked out.

"I'm not even tired," Amber grumbled. She knew she should feel bad for mouthing off, but her mother was so good at making things up, the least she could do was *pretend* she had better ideas. Beetle must have been thinking the same thing.

"Maybe the fairies can help." He leaned forward and flopped back on the beanbag with a crunching sound.

Amber was about to tell him to stop when she saw the flash. It happened quickly, but it triggered a sense of déjà vu.

"Say that again," Amber demanded.

"Maybe the fairies can help," Beetle said repeating the flop.

Another flash. Beetle's eyes were closed so he wouldn't have seen it.

Perhaps Amber's room was being watched after all. Maybe a secret camera was taking pictures. Or a drone hovered outside. Amber didn't spot anything hovering by the window, and the flash didn't seem to have a direct source. But what caused it? Beetle flopping while talking about fairies? Information seemed to be blowing past her like a balloon on a windy day, and she needed to grab the string before it disappeared.

Sandra returned. "Come on, Beetle. Get those teeth brushed, and I'll tuck you in." Beetle scuttled past. She paused, studying Amber's face. "The best thing for now is to keep our imaginations active and our minds open until we're shown a sign, okay?"

Amber nodded. She wasn't sure if the light flash counted as a sign but decided to keep her observation to herself. She might sound foolish if she shared it. Or make it go away. As if whatever was controlling this universe would stash the idea (or her!) in a dungeon.

Sandra closed the door. Amber picked up Lion and renewed her pacing.

In books, portals always led to worlds with *more* magic, not less. Trying to figure out when the two worlds might touch seemed as likely as driving around in search of a house when you didn't have the address; something Amber had experienced firsthand after her mother forgot to bring Amber's invitation to a classmate's seventh birthday party and circled the neighborhood in search of balloons or a familiar child going in. Amber could still picture herself in the back seat, dressed in her best outfit, clutching the kitten puzzle her mother had picked up from the Dollar Store. They didn't find the house, Amber missed the party, and the consolation prize of keeping the puzzle was marred by the fact that it was short three pieces.

Their current situation felt just like trying to put together that puzzle. Setting down limited pieces toward an impossible goal. Had Amber really thought they could just walk back home through the School Towel Service building? It seemed foolish now. It wasn't like they could camp out in front of it waiting for a glimpse of the Parallels, for surely a camera drone would spot them, or they'd be picked up for missing the buzzer schedule, and then what? Trouble with a capital *T*. And there didn't seem to be any guarantee that a touchpoint would happen elsewhere unless the Parallels wanted to come back too. Like that would happen.

"Stick with the pieces you do have, Amber," she told herself. There still might be enough to get a clearer picture. So Beetle mentioned the fairies and the light shifted. The other time Amber had noticed this, she'd said something to her mother. What was it? Oh yeah, it was in the bedroom when she'd brought up the witch returning her mother's keys. But did it mean anything?

She wanted to consult with Lion, but now she worried about drones with microphones. Or maybe the egg cameras were recording sound even when they were closed. She hugged him to her chest. How could her mother sleep at night, knowing she was being spied on? Sandra was right about the similarities back home though. Clara and Debbie always charged their phones next to their beds while they slept, and their "helpful" home systems seemed to know everything about their habits.

She pulled Lion closer. *At least they can't see into my brain. Think, Amber, think.*

But all she could think about was how her mother's example was wrong. It wasn't two trains running next to each other; instead, it was a person trying to run on foot alongside an airplane in mid-flight. What if they were stranded here for months? Even if time moved more slowly at home, she might still miss the entire softball season. She couldn't imagine what the other Amber would do in her place. She didn't seem like the type who'd try to fake playing. She'd probably lie and fake an injury instead.

Amber wished there were some way to know what the date was back home. Out of habit she pressed the button on her watch to flash it to the date screen. It still showed the date they'd left, THURS MARCH 30, like a clock smashed at the scene of a crime. Of course, what was she expecting? If the watch battery was slowing down, why would the date track? She switched back to the time. The digital numbers made her think of a game clock paused at 6:59:59 p.m. She was about to lower her arm when she caught a flicker from the watch face. Now it read 7:00:00. She looked away. Looked back. Just in case she'd imagined it. Still 7:00:00, and the seconds had paused as before.

An idea came. The kind that arrives when you leave the windows of your mind open. She could hear her mother complete the saying, "You just never know what might fly in." Sandra had experienced two weeks to Amber's two days. What if the watch wasn't broken after all? What if instead it was tracking, as it always had, the slower passing of time in their real world? Should she even dare to imagine this?

But then the day's final buzzer buzzed, the lights turned out, and Amber was left imagining her way in the dark.

14

The next morning Amber added another *D* word to her list of adjectives. *Distracted.* Sandra's braid had been done haphazardly, her shirt was on inside out, and the meal bore all the signs of inattentiveness. Undercooked eggs. Toast burned and flipped so the brown side faced down. No juice or berries. Amber forced a few bites. It must have been enough, because when Sandra checked their numbers she said, "Up 10 percent in all areas. Good. Maybe they won't watch us as closely today." She glanced up at the closed egg camera but still dropped her voice. "I gave it some thought and I think it's worth another stab at the School Towel Service building. Even if getting through is as likely as finding a golden ticket." (The one type of reference Sandra always seemed to get right was anything related to a children's book.)

"How?" Amber asked. She'd decided not to say anything just yet about the watch. She wanted more time to, as her mother had put it, muddle things over. That morning the digital numbers had only advanced three minutes. She found this reassuring, even if her theory turned out to be as wishful as talking to fairies. "Don't you have to get off the bus before we drive by?"

Sandra motioned them closer and whispered the plan. The buzzer went off. They raced to get their school things as Sandra fixed her shirt. They reached the door just as the egg camera opened.

Amber wondered if the monitor would pick up on their nervous energy. She sensed it in the air, like the anticipation she felt before a softball tournament, that mix of excitement and worry. They were going to the School Towel Service building! Even if it didn't work out—oh, but please, please let it!—how re-energizing it was to have a goal. In her stomach she felt a chipping away of the concrete, as a faint beam of light leaked through, bringing with it a sense of hope. They might escape this world today!

⸙

They waited alone at the bus stop. Beetle brought his arms in and out of his shirt, as if training for an event. Which in many ways, he was. After they boarded, they walked toward the back to an empty row on the correct side. Beetle slid in first and squeezed to the window to make room, twisting his arms back inside his shirt. When the bus reached the mothers' stop, Beetle called out that he was stuck. Sandra, as planned, wrestled to extract his arms, while the rest of the women disembarked. There seemed to be fewer of them today, and the bus was soon on the move.

Sandra said with exaggerated alarm, "Oh no, I've missed my stop."

Beetle wrapped his newly freed arms around his torso, as if offering a consoling hug, and softly counted down the blocks. "Four. Three. Two."

Amber's skin tingled. Would this be it? The plan was simple. As soon as they saw themselves in the window, they would hold hands and make a joint wish to go back home. Could that be all it took? Amber imagined herself heading to school in her mother's smelly car, with this whole miserable adventure behind them. She would never EVER stop appreciating what she had. Or forget how easily a familiar routine could get stolen.

Sandra gasped. "No."

Amber saw the crane before she saw the building. Or at least the half of the building that was still standing. Swinging from the arm of the crane was a wrecking ball.

"This can't be," Sandra said.

But it was.

As the bus passed, three startled faces stared at the shell of what was once the School Towel Service building. The window had been removed, and through the frame Amber saw only dirt and rubble, as if the front had been nothing but a stage set. An illusion. The wrecking ball swung back, and Amber turned away. Her stomach clenched. The cracks resealed. This couldn't be happening. This was not happening. Their one gateway back. Was it the Parallels? Had they wished for this to happen so they could stay where they were? Or maybe Sandra was wrong. Maybe the universe wanted to capture them instead, like an animal in a trap.

Beetle whimpered and Sandra, still with a look of disbelief, reached up and pushed the call button for an unscheduled stop. The bus lurched and she rose.

"What are we going to do?" Amber grabbed her mother's arm. She needed to hear that everything was going to be okay. She needed to hear that this wasn't their only shot.

Sandra didn't meet her gaze. In a low voice that seemed to be directed as much to herself as to Amber, she said, "We'll figure it out. There's never only one solution. We'll find another way." Then with an annoyed call from the driver to "hurry up," Sandra rushed down the aisle.

School was just as awful as the day before. The class lessons were ridiculous. And it took Amber an exhausting amount of effort to blend in, although she offered only the slightest of nods in response to the barrage of "that's dumb" and "you're stupid." But when Debbie called one of the smaller boys in the class a shrimp, Amber blurted out, "He's fun-sized."

"What's your problem, Amber?" Debbie asked with a shake of her head. "Since when did you become *nice*?" She said it like it was a curse word.

At recess, Amber tried to sneak into the library again, but

the doors were closed for a staff meeting. She went outside to the field and joined Debbie and Clara as they watched the boys toss a football.

"Don't you wish you could play too?" Amber asked.

"That's dumb. Football is dangerous," Clara responded. "I'm not getting a tooth knocked out."

Amber offered a half-hearted "No, you're dumb," feeling like an actor reading from a teleprompter. "Well, what about a foot race then or a game of catch?"

"You mean to get their attention?" Debbie asked. She tilted her head toward the boys on the field, then smiled as Jimmy Andrews caught the ball in front of them.

Clara snorted. "The only attention you'd get for that is from Mr. P."

She motioned to the gym teacher standing guard by the entrance to the field. That's when Amber spotted the security cameras, perched on three of the posts, like resting sparrows.

A few yards away, Jimmy and Keith skirmished over the ball. Soon they were on the ground, throwing punches.

"Go, Jimmy," Debbie yelled.

"Keith, you're such a loser," yelled Clara.

Amber forced herself to join in the cheer. In her mind, her voice sounded more like the scream of a person trapped in a horror film. And that horror film was her life.

~

That night at dinner, no matter how hard they forced themselves to be positive, Sandra, Amber, and Beetle had lost all their morning pep. As Beetle was playing with his water glass, he knocked it over, sopping the basket of bread and Amber's macaroni.

Sandra snapped, "Beetle, what are you doing? Look at this mess."

Then she flinched and tried to smile as she mopped up the spill with her napkin. "Now, Bernard, please try to be more careful with your glass." But the egg camera saw all. It was clear from Sandra's expression after dinner that their numbers weren't good.

Amber's helplessness felt like a backpack weighted down with math books. She barely had the energy for her English homework, which shouldn't have required much, since it was just writing sentences using spelling words. The words weren't hard, but she found it challenging to craft sentences that wouldn't offend, after her first failed attempts:

What I do is none of your business. I can't ascertain what's going on with these rules. The government is not benevolent.

She also had to correct an essay that had been written by the other Amber, who, among other grammatical errors, tended to confuse *your* and *you're*. Amber had been known to get lazy on that usage too. It almost made her feel connected to this other self. But when she thought of the other girl sleeping in her bed, and getting access to softball and freedom, she felt tempted to mess up on purpose, which, she realized, if she stayed trapped here, would not be *advantageous*.

She checked her watch in case it offered some new clue. The time had moved up an hour but she didn't have enough data to figure out a pattern. After the disappointment at the School Towel Service, she decided it was best to just assume the watch was broken.

At lights out Amber crawled into bed, hoping sleep would provide an escape. Maybe she'd wake up and find out the entire thing had been a bad dream. That she'd been concussed from a softball. Or had opened the hall closet and been knocked out by one of the broken appliances Sandra had stuck in there until she could take it to be recycled. Which, of course, she never did. Amber drifted off to this fantasy, and when she woke up the next morning she thought it might be true. But then she spotted the perfectly aligned bulletin board. She threw a pillow at it but missed. She couldn't even throw straight anymore! She tossed off the covers. Feeling defiant, she put on the dirty clothes she'd worn on the day she arrived. Her *other world* outfit. On her way to the bathroom, she swiped her hand over the bulletin board so it looked as though a brisk wind had blown through. As the buzzer sounded, she unpinned the photo strip and dropped it in the trash.

15

At breakfast, the meal was cooked properly but the portions were smaller. Only enough eggs for two. The heels of bread. A few strawberry halves floated in what looked like watery ketchup. Amber noticed her mother wasn't wearing her PFA shirt. As soon as the camera closed, Sandra twisted her braid up and stuck it under a hat with a wide brim. She looked almost as ridiculous as her doppelgänger in the baseball cap. When Amber asked what was going on, Sandra coughed into her fist.

"Taking a sick day. Seem to have caught a cold."

Sandra rarely got sick. Something she attributed to her vegetarian diet and a daily dose of apple cider vinegar with garlic, which Amber found grosser than any real medicine. But Sandra did look tired, and there were likely new microbes here, something that their other-world's white blood cells wouldn't know how to attack.

"Will you guys be okay on the bus by yourselves?"

"Well, duh, we're not babies." The snarky tone boosted Amber's confidence, like a verbal shield.

"I know that."

Sandra put her hand on Amber's hair, and Amber didn't push it off. Underneath her mother's lined face, there was a look of real fear, as if she were heading out to meet a dragon or walking into the eye of a storm. "Where are you going today?" Amber asked, trying to block the fear in her own voice.

Sandra checked to make sure the camera was still closed. "I can't give you specifics, but you were right. We can't just sit around waiting. There's someone I need to talk to, someone who might make things here more bearable while we look for another way back. I should be here when you get home, but if not, I'll leave the door unlocked, and you'll need to get creative with the buzzers. You can do that, right?" Amber nodded. Beetle popped out from his shirt and nodded too. "Great. Now let's get these dishes put away."

The strawberry bowl hadn't been touched. Sandra picked it up and stuck it in the fridge while Amber carried the dishes, including her mother's empty one, to the sink. She was surprised that her mother knew someone who might help. Why hadn't she reached out sooner? But just like yesterday, it felt better to have a plan. And her mother's mention of creativity reminded Amber that after so many years of training their imaginations, the three of them might have a special skill that could serve them well in this world.

~

Again, Amber and Beetle were the only ones at the bus stop. The sky was its usual yellowish gray. There were puddles on the ground and patches of mud.

Amber grabbed Beetle's shirt to keep him from trying to leap over the puddles, since he was often known to miss. Even though they were the only ones standing there, she felt exposed and kept checking overhead for another one of the Squirrel UFO drones.

She realized she couldn't remember what it was like not to see that yellow-tinted sky, or how it had felt when she'd first arrived, when the ground seemed aslant. Hopefully what was happening was like climbing a mountain and adjusting to the new atmosphere. That was okay, because you just re-adjusted going down. But what if being in this world was more like colored dye soaking into fabric? If they stayed too long would they be permanently stained? Permanently altered?

Amber longed to do jumping jacks. Or run really fast to the tree and back. Or leap a puddle (she was much better than Beetle at staying dry). Anything to keep her mind from being the only thing to race.

The white bus turned the corner and pulled up to the stop with a belch of exhaust. As Amber and Beetle tried to board, the bus driver, the same woman from the other days, stopped them. "Where's your mother?" the driver demanded.

"Sick," Amber answered automatically.

"Well then, she should have hired a sitter to take you."

"But I'm twelve." Amber straightened in case her slouch had made her look younger.

"Under fourteen requires direct adult supervision."

Amber just stared. Didn't the driver understand the insanity of this? The bus was headed straight to their school! Amber saw two other kids from her school already on board, a third-grade girl and Stuart Matthews. And it wasn't like the mothers even rode all the way to school anyway.

"So you're not going to take us to school?" Amber heard the snarkiness in her tone. Surely the driver making them miss school was something the PFA would not approve of.

"I can't let you on without an adult. It's the rule."

Amber felt her temper flare. The driver looked smug. She probably hated kids and lived only for making their lives miserable. But Amber also felt worried. If they went home, would the PFA check on them with a site visit? If so, and their mother wasn't there, what would happen?

"Please," Amber pleaded.

"I'll supervise," a woman's voice called from the back of the bus. One of Stuart's mothers, the one Amber didn't know as well, came down the aisle. She had taken out her card and was waving it toward the driver.

The driver seemed to consider this, then gestured irritably for them to board. Amber and Beetle scrambled up the stairs, the doors closing with a *whoosh* behind them, almost snapping the clasp off Beetle's backpack.

Stuart's mother motioned Amber and Beetle to follow her to the back of the bus, then slid into an empty row. Beetle slid in next to her, and Amber sat next to Stuart.

"Your mother must really be sick," Stuart's mother said. She was expressionless, her braid pulled tautly, as if stretching her face into a blank canvas.

"She is," Amber lied, trying to look solemn, which wasn't hard. The run-in with the driver had unnerved her. There were so many rules, and each one seemed more ridiculous than the last. What other crazy thing would they come up with? Waiting until you're eighteen for a driver's license or an after-school job? (Sorry, Amber, those are already in place, although boys can get their licenses a year sooner, and anyone can buy a gun as soon as they turn sixteen.)

Stuart sat stiffly next to her. *Poor guy*, Amber thought. *Probably thinks I'm mean like the others.* And then she remembered that as far as he knew, she was. "So, you excited for school?" Amber asked.

Stuart's mother gestured that she should talk more quietly.

"I don't know," Stuart answered.

Amber tried again. "Is your other mother at work?"

Amber knew Ms. Marlene because she'd coached Amber's third-grade softball team. Ms. Marlene worked in an animal shelter, and she and Amber's mother would sometimes chat about animal rights.

Stuart turned pale and gave his mother a look. She grabbed Amber's arm, put her face close. Her breath smelled of peppermint and coffee. "What did you say?"

Amber tried to pull away. "I was just asking about Ms. Marlene. I thought she might be at work since she wasn't on the bus."

Stuart and his mother exchanged another look. His mother looked around nervously, although the bus was emptier than it had been the day before, and no one was seated nearby.

"I don't know where you're getting your information. Stuart has only one mother, and that's me. Got it?" Her grip on Amber's arm was starting to hurt, but her expression was one of terror, not anger.

"Got it." Amber wrenched free. "I was wrong, sorry." She turned to face forward but not before she saw Stuart swipe his eyes with his sleeve.

They rode the rest of the way in silence, which gave Amber time to study the other families. There were definitely fewer passengers today. The kids who had asked about the farm the day before were missing. Maybe they'd gotten their wish. When the bus stopped at the business district, the remaining mothers kissed their children and filed off.

Stuart's mother leaned over and whispered something in his ear. She gave Amber a sharp look and headed down the aisle. Amber moved over to sit next to Beetle. He had stuck himself against the side of the bus like a piece of gum. Amber looked out the window and spotted a tall building at the end of the block. It was one of those chrome high-rises that her mother had complained about as the most unimaginative type of architectural design. Women in white shirts streamed through the front door. That must be the building her mother called the Structure.

She thought of her mother in that building, reading other people's emails, and about the people who had to screen the camera footage. Sandra had taught Amber to look at issues from all directions, so she tried to imagine that some of the workers in the Structure cared about the families, that they believed the cameras stopped abusive adults and gave kids a better chance to thrive, that they were people who believed they were doing good work. Amber wondered what would happen in that building if the egg camera turned on tonight and her mother wasn't home. Would an alarm sound? Would the police be summoned? Now she wished her mother was at work doing as she'd been told...that they'd followed the rules.

No! This was what happened when fear took over. The important thing, Amber told herself, was to not draw any unnecessary attention that day at school.

Unfortunately, that choice wasn't entirely up to her.

16

Mr. P. came for her during social studies. Amber had been seated in the back, tuning out the non-history history lesson, when he walked in and whispered in the teacher's ear. Amber noticed the other kids straighten and stare ahead.

"Amber, please take your things and go with Mr. Purchett."

Amber felt her face burn. Was it because she'd made that comment in science class? Or maybe they found out she'd looked up Darwin on a school computer. She felt shaky but forced herself to walk tall and hold her head high.

"Follow me," Mr. P. said.

She kept her gaze on the tight pull of fabric across Mr. P.'s back. At her other school, he'd been well liked, although he made them do way too many sit-ups. But he always treated girls and boys the same, and she appreciated that. Maybe he'd been demoted for that reason. Or maybe there wasn't PE anymore. They hadn't had PE the past few days, and she hadn't thought to check ahead on her schedule. Usually she went to the gym twice a week. She could ask Mr. P. about it, but given his current demeanor, she expected it would be a one-sided conversation.

"Clear out your locker, leave the textbooks," Mr. P. instructed.

Again Amber did as she was told, abandoning her math and not-even-actual-science textbooks, then followed him around the corner to the service elevator. He pushed the down button. They waited in tense silence. The old Mr. P. would have offered up encouraging reminders to "keep her chin up" and "look on the bright side."

Amber gripped the straps of her backpack. If she was in trouble, the school would certainly call her mother and find out she wasn't at home sick. What about Beetle? He'd be so scared if he went to the bus after school and she wasn't there. Maybe she could ask to stop by his classroom to let him know, although what she really wanted to do was grab Beetle's hand and run, run, run as fast as they could, out of this school and all the way home. The classic fight-or-flight response. And a waste of time. Someone or something would be waiting for them, of course. A drone. A police officer. A van. And it wasn't like there was any hope to be found by going to the School Towel Service building, although she wondered if they'd given up too easily. Maybe the location provided the portal, not the physical window. Maybe all they needed was the reflective surface of a puddle or a leftover shard of glass.

The elevator doors dinged opened, and Mr. P. motioned for her to step inside.

Even if Amber was correct about not needing the building, the Parallels might still have to be nearby for the touchpoint to work. And if her mother really had been here for two weeks, how would they ever be able to coordinate the timing? One of Sandra's mangled clichés came to mind—"Like finding a needle in a flower bed."

She glanced at her watch. The time read eight thirty a.m. That was quite a leap. She pushed the button to check the date. FRI MARCH 31. Did broken watches ever jump ahead in time? She couldn't figure out what might have caused the change. But if—and this was a very, very big if—the watch time was correct, then that meant the other Amber and Beetle would just be starting first period at school, except a day after they'd switched places, while Amber had journeyed weeks ahead. Dizzy, she leaned against the wall and closed her eyes. She'd always felt claustrophobic in elevators, especially old ones that creaked and moved so slowly. The image of the fairy godmother from their morning drives came to mind, wearing her crazy hat and those filthy gardening shoes. Amber heard her speak in the voice her mother ascribed to her, *You've answered your own question about timing, haven't you?*

"How?" The word slipped out. Amber startled to hear her voice in the tight space.

"Quiet." Mr. P. glared.

The doors slid open. They were at the basement level of the school, where the locker rooms and PE office were located.

"Out," Mr. P. said.

Amber, even in her anxious state, suppressed the urge to remind him to "say please."

Off the elevator, he turned right. It appeared they were headed to the girls' locker room.

A new idea flew in, so obvious that Amber had to keep herself from saying "Aha!" The fairy godmother was right. Amber had answered her own question about timing. Fridays, first period, Amber had PE. Students were given ten minutes at the beginning of class to change into their gym uniforms, which meant if the watch was correct (and she wasn't buying it yet), then she and the other Amber might be in the locker room at the same time! In science Ms. Stein always spoke about how trial and error was one of the best ways to reach a solution. Here was a chance for Amber to put her watch theory to the test.

As expected, Mr. P. pointed to the door to the locker room. "Wait in there. I'll be down the hall. No monkey business."

Amber flashed on what "no monkey business" would have meant in her other world—gossip, stealing each other's gym shoes, and giggles behind open palms.

She followed his command and tried to disguise her eagerness. The sign next to the locker room had been covered up. Instead of *Girls' Locker Room*, it read *Girls' Holding.* So this must be "the pen." The locker room looked the same, with fluorescent lighting, cinderblock walls, and green lockers. But instead of smelling of bleach and sweat, it smelled damp and musty, like an unused basement.

Out of habit she went to her locker, number 192. Remnants of Scotch tape were stuck to the door. Amber wondered if the kids here still decorated their friends' lockers for birthdays. She remembered how good it felt to enter the locker room on her last birthday and discover blue streamers cascading over signs that read *Amber Rocks* and *Happy Bday BFF* in silver bubble letters. The cleaning crew took the signs down that night, as they did for any unauthorized items affixed to school property, but Amber had stored the picture in her memory, what Sandra called a brain photo. Amber couldn't think of anything from the last few days that she wanted to turn into a brain photo, but they seemed to be forming against her will—the fearful look on her mother's face that morning; the wrecking ball at the School Towel Service building; Stuart's stiff figure on the bus.

On a corner locker, she noticed writing scratched into the metal. She came closer and read, *Six hours and counting.* On another locker: *If you read this and I'm gone, remember me and keep fighting on. JJ.*

Amber wasn't surprised to see that the JJ in this world might have ended up in the pen. The JJ at Amber's real school was president of the Student Council and was always circulating petitions. These were mostly for things Amber agreed with, like less testing, better communication, and the need for gender-neutral bathrooms, although she'd skipped the one calling for an all-vegan lunchroom. Amber started to look for other messages, but then she remembered her plan. She hurried through the adjoining door to the bathroom, not that she needed to rush. The time on her watch hadn't changed.

She walked over to the row of sinks and stood in front of the first mirror. It was cracked in two places, so she centered her reflection between the lines. "Hello, Amber." When she waved, her image waved too. She leaned in to study herself more closely. Some hair had sprung loose from her ponytail and her skin seemed gray in the fluorescent lighting, but everything appeared a perfect match to what she thought she looked like.

She moved to the next mirror. "Hello, Amber."

Already she doubted her impulse. Was she really going off the advice of a figment of her imagination? But that's what made this plan seem legitimate—if, as her mother had suggested, imagination was their greatest ally.

The door to the locker room squeaked open and a new voice, brusque and female, called, "When you're through in there, sit on a bench. I'll be back for you. You're a lucky girl to have such a short wait." The door squeaked shut.

Lucky? Amber didn't feel lucky. She needed more time, not less. What to do? She heard the fairy godmother's voice again, this time with a tinge of impatience.

More effort, Amber. What do you want to see?

"I want to see the Parallel me," Amber answered.

An exasperated sigh. *So what are you waiting for?*

Amber hadn't realized that the fairy godmother had an attitude. She'd have to say something to her mother about that.

Moving to the third sink, Amber leaned closer and peered into the mirror, as if trying to see the image behind the image, like one of those pixilated pictures with a picture hidden within. "Hello, Parallel Amber," she said with as much conviction as she could muster. She leaned back.

This time her reflection was like watching the replay of a video as the figure in the mirror leaned forward and tucked a loose hair into place, even though Amber stood so still she barely breathed. And her reflection was speaking. Amber could actually *hear* her speak!

"Well, I think the field trip sounds really dumb," the other Amber said.

Debbie's disembodied voice came from off-screen (off-mirror?). "I know. What's so great about seeing a bunch of stinky cows? My mother thinks it's a waste of school funds. Is your mother actually going to go?"

From another off-screen position came Clara's voice. "I bet she'll show up in overalls and a farmer's hat." She oinked like a pig.

Amber couldn't help herself. "That's rude."

A look of surprise crossed the face of Amber's Parallel. Was she responding to the insult, or had Amber's own voice traveled through time, space, and glass?

Another squeak of door. "You fall into a toilet or what?"

Amber turned to answer, "I'll be right out."

When she turned back, she was staring into her own tired image. She put her hand forward, felt the cold glass. Had she missed a touchpoint? Her first, and perhaps only, opportunity to switch back? She knew she wouldn't have taken it without Beetle. She could never leave him or her mother behind. "All for one and one for ice cream," she said softly. She used the bathroom—who knew when she'd get another chance—washed her hands, and walked back into the holding pen.

As the woman had noted, Amber was much luckier than her predecessors. Six hours in that stinky greenish room would have made anyone feel like a prisoner. Amber had to wait only a few more minutes before the woman reentered. She was older with short gray hair that sprang up as if she'd recently touched an electrical outlet. She wore a navy PFA shirt and carried a clipboard. "Follow me."

Amber didn't move. "What's going on? Where are you taking me?"

"You'll see when you get there, won't you? I suggest you start walking."

Amber wished she hadn't talked back. (Her mother had a cliché about that too, some vegetarian version of welcoming flies with honey.) She was working up the nerve to ask if they could possibly, if it wasn't too much bother, stop by the fourth-grade classroom. But there was no need. As they approached the elevator, a male guard exited the boys' locker room with Beetle in tow. Amber wanted to throw her arms around her little brother. He hated hugs but would not have been able to fend her off since his arms were tucked into his shirt as if he'd placed himself in handcuffs.

Amber was bursting to tell Beetle about what had just happened. She tried to think optimistically. If she'd found this one touchpoint, there would be others. It wasn't as if her other self would suddenly be sent on a safari or to boarding school. But she was equally worried about where they were being taken. She assumed they'd first have to go see the principal, who would call her mother, who wouldn't answer because she was off to who-knows-where. Then they'd get sent back to the holding pen or to an actual cell in the Structure. She found that she preferred the second option. With all those mothers around, surely nothing bad could happen. Hadn't Stuart's mother jumped in to help earlier? And she wasn't even all that nice. *Just keep it together*, Amber told herself. She felt that at any moment she might accidentally blurt out one of Kevin James's curse words. That was what her mother meant about how easy it was to make mistakes when you felt like you were constantly being watched and judged.

The two guards hustled Amber and Beetle into the elevator. She gave Beetle what she hoped was a reassuring smile. At least she knew he hadn't gotten in trouble for talking back.

"You think this is funny?" the male guard demanded.

They got off the elevator on the first floor. Amber thought again about the kids who'd been held in the pen for hours and hours. What could they have possibly done that deserved such harsh punishment? Amber was sure that wasn't putting kids first. How could it even be legal?

"You get the van. I'll check them out," Amber's guard

said. She headed into the office. Beetle's guard strolled out front.

When both were out of earshot, Amber whispered. "You okay, Bug?"

Beetle nodded. His look asked a whole bunch of questions that Amber didn't have answers for.

"I have something new to tell you," Amber said. "Did you see anything in the locker room? Anything unusual?"

Beetle shook his head and she imagined that he had likely kept his head tucked into his shirt the entire time.

The female guard came back, so Amber fell silent. Her update would have to wait.

Around them it seemed like a normal school day. In the office, the school secretary answered the telephone. The passing buzzer sounded, and kids flooded the hall on their way to their next class. A few gave side glances at Amber and Beetle, but most of them acted as if they weren't there. Mr. P. had returned to his stool and looked even more stiff than usual, probably due to the presence of the guards.

Through the front window, Amber saw a white van pull up. It looked like the one that had picked up the woman and her children from the building next door.

"Let's go," Amber's guard said.

Mr. P. nodded to the guard as they walked out. "Very glad to be of service," he said.

Amber's thoughts raced. Were they being taken to the Farm? How would their mother know where to find them? Unless she was already in the van. That would be a relief. After all, wasn't the point of the Farm to keep families together? But maybe they had a separate Farm for juvenile delinquents. There was still so much about this world that Amber didn't know, didn't understand. She should have spent more time in the school library. She should have asked Sandra more questions. How would they find another touchpoint if they were going someplace they'd never been? That question triggered a fragment of an idea, but she couldn't make her way to it. It was like trying to remember a dream. Each time she stepped closer, the idea seemed to take one step back.

When they climbed into the van, Amber saw they were the only passengers. "Where's our mother?" she asked.

This time the guards just ignored her. The van had a rank smell, like old milk, and there was an uncomfortable vibe, as if the air itself hummed with anxiety. Amber checked to make sure Beetle buckled his seat belt. She didn't want them to do anything else wrong. She still wasn't sure what they'd done, but whatever it was had created a flashing arrow pointed at their heads. The van pulled away, headed to a destination unknown. She realized she'd forgotten to buckle her own seat belt, and clicked it into place, hoping the guards didn't hear.

She thought again about how easy it was to make mistakes when you felt like you were being judged. That might explain why she'd always felt a little fake around Debbie and Clara, as if she already expected them to put her down or point out some personal failing. Which they often had, under the guise of pointers for self-improvement.

Sandra seemed to have noticed this too. "Looks like you send a lot of energy Clara and Debbie's way. Do you get anything back?" Amber had rolled her eyes. Because of course she got something back. She got attention, and a feeling of fitting in, of being someone important. The only time she'd felt that way before was when she played softball. Was that such a bad thing? But she was starting to understand that a lot of what she did for her friends meant trying to be the person she thought they wanted her to be. Just like she'd been trying to be the person this other world wanted her to be. And boy, was it exhausting. When she got back home, she'd be the one to reject Debbie and Clara and the group of wannabees.

It was time to make new friends, to be her own person.

She'd liked eating lunch with Sarika. When she got back maybe they could even hang out after school sometime. The copy editor in her brain adjusted the thought to "*if* you get home."

No! It had to be *when*. *If* was not an option. But the *how* banged against the borders of Amber's imagination, like a moth trapped in a room with no window or light.

In the front of the van the guards chatted about where they were going to eat lunch—the man wanted pizza, the woman a burger—and complained about their busy afternoon. Apparently several more pickups were scheduled for after-school hours.

"They seriously have to up the staff for this kind of sweep," the woman said.

On the radio a host shouted about "a moral crisis." Beetle's stomach grumbled so loudly Amber was surprised the guards didn't yell at them to keep it down. She wanted to give Beetle another reassuring smile but felt like she'd need a pulley and lever to get her lips to tilt up.

"I wish we could just pretend our way out of here," Beetle mumbled.

"I know, Little Bug. Me too."

"No talking," the female guard said.

We really are prisoners, Amber thought. She flashed back to a time her team had acted rowdy on the bus after a game and Coach Dee ordered them to stay silent for ten minutes. But then they really had been acting up. (Amber recalled the unpleasant challenge of trying to remove a spitball mixed with chewing gum out of her hair.) She almost looked forward to reaching their destination, because there was a chance that Sandra might be waiting for them there. But so what if she was? They still weren't any closer to getting home. If anything, with each development they were moving farther away. Amber's anxiety shifted into anger. Sandra should have worked harder to play by the rules. But wasn't it Amber who'd pushed her mother to take action? Now Amber was mad at herself too.

"Amber, I'm hungry. Can I eat my lunch?"

Beetle's voice was so soft that she understood him only by watching his lips.

It was probably close to lunch period at school. What time had she been pulled out of class? She started to glance at her watch but redirected her gaze to the digital clock on the dashboard. 11:55. Amber was too nervous to be hungry. She shook her head, worried that the guards would confiscate Beatle's lunch if he took it out, like the teachers in her old school did when kids tried to sneak food in class. (There had been rules at her old school too, but at least they made sense. Well, all except the one about no running in the halls, which seemed to contradict the rule about not being late for the bell. JJ had circulated a petition.)

Amber tried to open her mind to the possibility that they'd never get back. *Make lemonade from lemons* had been another (old) Mr. P. picker-upper. Amber tried to convince herself that not everything in this world was bad. The bus to and from school meant they were never late. And Sandra had a real job, unlike all the stringing together of positions she did at home. They never used to eat together as often. Plus, although this tactic of being pulled from school seemed extreme, maybe they really were going someplace better. Maybe the Farm was as it appeared, and her mother had gotten it wrong. She was still new here too.

The van screeched to a stop with a blast of its horn as a delivery truck cut across its path. Amber and Beetle lurched forward and back, and she was glad she'd remembered to buckle. The guards shouted some insults at the other driver, then proceeded. Amber looked out the window to keep from feeling sick.

The van was heading west. It was still so strange that the scenery could be familiar, even though so much about this place felt like a foreign land. They passed the high school, and the field where Amber had played her fourth-grade games, and the strip mall where she used to get her hair cut (if and when Sandra remembered to take her, and only after Amber put her foot down about her mother's uneven attempts to cut it at home). The stores at the strip mall seemed vacant, and Amber wondered if the mall was also in line for a wrecking ball. The rain had started again. Amber tapped along on her thigh to the *swish swish* of the windshield wipers. *It will all be okay*, she chanted silently to the rhythm, and for a few moments she felt a sense of calm.

She wondered if that's why people went along with the changes here. If you were always trying to see the good side of things, the unpleasant parts could slip by in the peripheries, like a sneaky shadow.

Amber had exceptional peripheral vision. That was one of the things that made her such a strong softball player. She could see the runner at second while her eyes were trained on home plate. She'd had hopes for high school varsity. Maybe a college scholarship. Even without playing on an overpriced travel team. She'd overheard Coach Dee say as much after the last tournament win. "That play's worth a college scout visit for sure." A lump formed in her throat. What good did that talent do her now?

Just past the outer boundaries of town, the van turned into the parking lot of an industrial complex. The back of the parking lot was filled with rows of white buses and vans. The building looked as if it was used to make things that were boring but necessary, like packing crates or batteries. There were several loading-dock bays, all empty. The van pulled around to the front of the building and stopped in front of two glass doors. This side also had a parking lot. A sign for *Employee Parking* pointed to an area with a smattering of cars. Another sign marked *Impound* pointed to a section that was nearly full. The cars in that section all looked as if they'd seen their share of miles. Next to the building entrance a tiny plot of unnaturally green grass was cordoned off with twine.

Amber's guard slid out of her seat and opened the back door. "Let's go."

Amber grabbed her backpack and nodded at Beetle to do the same. The sky was grayer than when they'd left school and seemed slightly thick, but any fresh air was better than the van smell.

The guard led them to the entrance. The grass appeared to be Astroturf. Two brittle plants flanked the doors. They'd been placed under the awning, out of the reach of the rain. It seemed cruel, and Amber wished she could push them into the open so they could have a drink. The guard hustled them through the doors toward a desk. A receptionist in a PFA shirt—young, maybe even college aged, her hair braided to the side—had been watching a bank of monitors. She looked up when the guard flashed a badge and waved them toward a set of steel doors. Amber smiled at her. She didn't smile back.

They entered a fluorescent-lit hallway lined with offices. It smelled of mildew and burnt coffee. Some of the doors were open, and Amber glanced in as they walked by. They seemed like normal offices with desks and filing cabinets, computers, and phones. One was occupied by a mustached man in a short-sleeved button-down. When he saw Amber looking, he shut the door.

At the end of the hall they met up with a second set of heavy doors. The guard pulled one open and motioned them through. The first thing to hit Amber was the noise. It sounded like an amplified playground. They walked into what must have once been the floor of a warehouse, but instead of machinery and shelving, it was filled with cots and lots and lots of children. Women, too, chasing and calling and sitting on cots as if to catch their breath. The space reminded Amber of the images on TV of shelters following a natural disaster. What were they all doing here?

But then Amber heard her name shouted in a familiar voice and saw a familiar figure running toward them. At that moment, Amber didn't care about anything in the world—this one or any other—only the feel of her mother's arms around her, pulling her into a hug.

17

Sandra kept an arm wrapped around each of their shoulders as she guided them down a row. She stopped next to three empty cots. "This is us."

The mattresses were covered in white sheets and scratchy-looking gray blankets. Amber saw their name masking-taped onto the metal frames of each bed. The middle cot had an indentation in the pillow, the blanket pulled askew.

"Home sweet home," Sandra said.

"I love what you've done with the décor." Amber tried to joke, but her voice sounded hollow.

"Where are we?" Beetle asked.

"Welcome to the Farm." Sandra gestured to the room.

"No, really," Amber said.

"Well, it's more like purgatory while they figure out where to put everyone." Sandra sank onto the cot. "Apparently they weren't prepared for the volume and are scrambling to add more long-term options."

Amber looked around. It seemed as if the cots went on forever. Many had items piled on top—jackets and clothes and stuffed animals. At the far end of the room, Amber saw women seated in rows of folding chairs. They watched a large-screen TV airing what looked like a news program. When she turned, she spotted another screen with the same program at the other end of the room. A baby cried and others joined in as if called into chorus.

"Where are the older kids?" Amber asked, realizing she and Beetle seemed to be the oldest ones in the room.

"They take them into another area for *schooling*." Sandra's tone implied that the education here followed a similar curriculum to the one Amber had been suffering through. To further her point she added, "Getting schooled in conformity, I assume."

The air felt warm and tight—the feel of so many bodies stuck in one space for an extended time. The smell was slightly better than the van, but Amber could imagine it deteriorating over time, like the locker room before and after a game. The locker room! Amber still needed to tell her mother and Beetle about what had happened there, how she had seen and heard the Parallel Amber in the mirror after hearing the fairy godmother's voice in her head. What if that had been her only shot after all? There was no way a touchpoint could happen if they were trapped in this not-anything-like-the-video Farm.

"Why are we here? Did you get caught doing something?"

Amber hadn't meant for her voice to sound so accusatory, but Sandra didn't seem to notice. She was busy prying Beetle out of his shirt. She studied his face. "They weren't rough with you, were they?" Beetle shook his head. Sandra seemed satisfied and let Beetle escape back into his cotton shell. She sat down and patted the blanket. "Why don't you both sit, and I'll explain what I can."

Beetle popped back out of his shirt. "I'm hungry."

Sandra sighed. "You missed lunch and dinner won't be for a while."

Beetle rustled into his backpack, pulled out his lunch bag, and waved it like a trophy.

"Ah, good news." She ruffled his hair and he let her.

Amber sat at the end of her mother's cot. "Did the PFA bring us here because you weren't giving us good food options?"

"Of course not." Sandra shook her head. "I mean the meals are part of the algorithm, but that's really just a gloss-over item."

"Algorithm?"

"I thought your generation were all tech whizzes. It's how

the PFA has been figuring out who should be inspected. The algorithm pulls up names and then the PFA officials review the footage and issue penalties. Now with so many new regulations and more families getting flagged, they've started enlisting other departments. I learned yesterday that my department, Communications, had been reassigned to screen footage starting today, and I was chatting with a woman here who'd been in Research. She told me they've been checking footage for over a week."

"So the mothers in the Structure are ratting on other mothers?" Amber asked, dismayed. "You would have done that?"

Sandra laid her hand on top of Amber's hand. Amber pulled it out of reach.

"It's not that simple. The women are scared. They're thinking of their children, about what might happen if they don't comply. What do you do if your food vouchers are cut off? Or you get demoted to a factory job that doesn't cover your rent? Turns out those rumors about the sweeps are true. We saw that with our own eyes. And to answer your question, no, I wasn't planning to rat on other mothers. It's one of the reasons I didn't go to work today."

"But the Farm is better than here, right?" Beetle asked.

Sandra shook her head. "That's the other thing I've picked up on. No one here will be heading to an *actual* farm. I was right about the overcrowding. Now they're routing everyone to the factories with some sort of tenement-style housing. Here we go, back to the dawn of the industrial age."

A boy ran by, chased by a younger girl who squealed in delight.

Amber watched them go. "You still haven't told us why you were brought here."

"Well, I'm sure my job avoidance would have landed us here eventually, but I was already on-site."

"Why?" Amber asked.

Beetle had finished one half of his sandwich and was starting on the other. Amber's stomach grumbled, but she had no interest in her own lunch. She knew it would be as hard to swallow as that day in the lunchroom when Leanne took her chair and she'd been doused in water. She'd much rather be there now. Even the soaked jeans would be welcome.

Sandra looked over her shoulder, as if to check for eavesdroppers. "I thought I could get a meeting with the man who runs this facility."

"Why would he meet with *you*?" Amber asked skeptically.

"I thought he'd see me because I know him. Or at least the version of him that lived in our world, and all the indicators suggest that some part of that relationship is still true."

"What relationship?" Amber was always reading about characters in books narrowing their eyes. She tried that now, although it just felt like squinting. The idea that her mother could be associated with one of the awful men in charge of this horrible place seemed even more traitorous than spying.

The running kids zoomed by a second time.

Sandra fluffed a pillow. Set it back down. Gave it another fluff. "This is going to be hard to tell you after so much time. I realize now I should have been more honest with you earlier, but, well, he's not a part of our lives anymore so it just never seemed urgent."

Amber could tell her mother was delaying something. Something big. "What?" she demanded. "It's not like he's our father or anything."

Sandra looked up and tried to take Amber's hand again. Amber put it behind her back. "You can't be serious!"

Her mother hushed her. Beetle stared at them, the last bite of sandwich bulging his cheek like a squirrel's.

Sandra shook her head. "This requires a lot of information that you don't have. I was waiting until I thought you'd be old enough to understand, but I probably would have kept pushing that date because—" She trailed off and reached for Amber's other hand. Amber brought it behind her back to join the first. Sandra clasped her own hands instead and pointed them toward Amber in a sign of supplication.

"Well, to be honest, it was easier not to tell you."

Amber didn't know what to say. Thoughts stomped through her mind, but one stomped the loudest. Somewhere in this very building their father was letting these terrible things happen to them, or at least the version of them that lived here. All these years she'd let herself believe her mother's excuse that he was off on some sort of gallant secret mission. Amber was no fan of fairy tales—the feeble girl with the tiny waist saved by the handsome prince, *blech!*—yet she'd created one for herself, it seemed. One that included a tall, bearded knight in shining armor riding in to announce, "Dad's home!" Now the image changed to a man riding off into the distance. Leaving them behind. Without a second glance or a care about their welfare.

A baby cried. Then another. A boy and girl zoomed by a third time, like train cars on a circular track.

"How did you know he was here?" Amber demanded.

She fought the urge to join the kids in their meaningless race. She reminded herself that the man here wasn't their actual father. But so many windows in her mind had flown open at the same time. She wanted to shut them until she could think more clearly.

"I saw him in one of the videos they make us watch at night. This one was about how they were addressing the higher demand for PFA Support Services. Of course, the program made it sound like this place was more country club than warehouse."

"So you came to ask our sort-of father for a meeting, thinking what? That he must have been our father here too?"

"Well, given that you exist, it would stand to both reason and biology."

Sandra paused while a PFA guard strolled by. The guard's gaze rested on them, then moved on.

Amber dropped her eyes. Had the guard been ordered to watch out for them, or keep watch? That probably depended on how well Sandra had impersonated the other mother. (As if the past few days hadn't proven how impossible a challenge that was.) Could Amber and Beetle impersonate their other selves well enough to be convincing? It occurred to her that she didn't really know anything about her Parallel self, just assumptions based on her Parallel's haughty look and popularity, although Amber had certainly picked up on some tips from trying to fool Debbie and Clara. Did the other Amber know about her father or had she also been left in the dark? Maybe the other Amber resented her own mother too, just for entirely different reasons. Amber had been so certain that she had the other girl pegged without giving much thought to why she'd gotten that way. She wished she had some way to communicate with her other self, like a pocket mirror that worked as a telephone between parallel worlds.

After the guard cleared their row, Sandra continued. "He was surprised to see me. Apparently, my other version had an arrangement that brought with it certain protections. He dismissed me quickly. On my way out I was stopped by a guard and brought here. They told me they were getting you, so I decided it was best to follow the trash-can rule."

Amber watched for the kids to make another pass, but they must have gotten tired. "So what did we do wrong? Why are we being kept here?"

"We aren't," Sandra said. "Not technically. We can walk out at any time." She gestured to the room. "All these women can. But then what? They don't have homes to go to or a car to get there. Their jobs are reliant on the PFA and doing what they're told. At least here there's community, and you've been promised three meals a day and a roof over your head. Your kids are safe and occupied. They even have a doctor on site. And you're led to believe that once you reach the next location, you'll have ongoing employment and security. The woman who was in Research said the PFA is training the kids for factory work with guaranteed jobs down the road. Although, of course, they'll become just another cog in the industrial wheel. But what would you do?"

"I'd go underground," Amber said.

Sandra shook her head. Her face darkened. "You're young and idealistic but you don't understand what it's like. Not just here, but at home too. It's not so easy when people depend on you, and you have to choose between ideals and food." She motioned to the room again. "Or integrity versus shelter."

The blare of a buzzer. Amber had grown so used to the sound she didn't even flinch. Doors slammed opened and the older children flooded in. It sounded like any school letting out for the day—laughter, shouts across the room, the echo of a basketball against the floor.

"Can you help me?" a woman asked.

It was a mother from a few cots down carrying a baby.

"I need to find my son. He may not remember where we are. We were just brought in this morning. Would you be able to watch her?" She motioned to the sleeping infant in her arms. "I'll be back quick."

"Of course," Sandra said. She smiled and took the swaddled infant.

Amber realized that for all her complaining about her mother she could not recall Sandra ever turning away from an act of kindness. But Amber couldn't shake the accusatory tone from her voice. "So what are we going to do now? Give up and go work in some factory somewhere?"

"I didn't say that." Sandra flashed Amber a look while gently rocking the baby. "Remember those touchpoints? I still believe they exist. We just need to stay open." Her look softened. "And one thing I know about you, Ember, is that you never give up, so don't let me hear you talking that way now."

Amber nodded. Now she felt ashamed. This must be what was meant by an emotional roller coaster. An emotional fun house was more like it, full of dark tunnels and rooms of mirrors.

Mirrors! "There was one at school," she exclaimed, "a touchpoint."

Trying to keep her mind from racing ahead of her voice, she filled her mother and Beetle in on as many of the details as she could remember, starting with the realization that her watch might be keeping time back home, up until the interaction with her Parallel self at the locker room mirror. "So maybe we should try to get back there."

Sandra shook her head. "If you tried to walk in during a school day, they'd block you, and me for sure. And even if we managed to sneak into the locker room somehow, there's little chance any sort of touchpoint would be activated."

Amber looked at her blankly.

"What I mean is the best we could hope for is that your other self would show up there. But Beetle and I would just be staring at our actual reflections. Unless they're trying to switch back too. Which is unlikely." The infant's eyes fluttered open. Sandra cooed softly and the baby settled back to sleep. "That means we need to look for one that will have all three of them present at the same time."

Amber stood and paced. She circled their cots like the zooming children, but on a tighter track. A young girl watched from a few cots down. Amber lengthened her steps and swung her arms, as if she were wading through a bog. The girl giggled until she was shushed by her mother.

Amber tried to focus on the problem. *Think. Think.* There was something that she was missing. As she swung to walk back the other way, she stuck her hands into her pockets and felt a slip of paper. She pulled it out. It was the stupid flyer for the field trip to the dairy farm, with a picture of a smiling cow, instructions for where parents and children should report, and a note that siblings were encouraged to attend. She felt her throat tighten over this item from her old world, as if she'd found Lion stuffed in her pocket, and not something that had initially filled her with dread. She started to walk again. Stopped. Checked the date. SATURDAY, APRIL 1. She checked her watch. Still MARCH 31. If her watch was to be believed—and she really, really wanted to believe—then the field trip was the next day.

She scanned the ceiling. As far as she could tell, there were no cameras, egg or otherwise. She strolled to her mother's cot and set the flyer face down on the blanket. Sandra gave her a quizzical look. Amber tried to keep her voice even, even though she wanted to squeal like the little girl from before.

"Touchpoint."

The mother of the infant returned, dragging a boy around Beetle's age.

"Why can't I hang out by the TVs?" he whined.

"Because I said so," the woman said.

She and Sandra traded sympathetic eyebrow lifts as Sandra returned the sleeping baby.

The boy seemed set to argue his case, but another buzzer sounded, followed by an announcement on a scratchy speaker system about dinner procedures and what television programs would air that evening. Some names were called to report with their belongings to the front, and Amber saw a few families gather up their things, yelling to each other to hurry, as if they'd lose their chance if they didn't get there fast.

"The grass is always greener in another industrial complex," Sandra muttered. She picked up the flyer and studied it. "I know where this is. It's not far from that awful poultry plant. I took you to a protest there when you were around four, remember?"

Amber gave her a "yeah right" look, although she did flash on an image of waving signs and a woman wearing a hat with a dangling ribbon. Likely it was just her imagination jumping in, or maybe she really did save a brain photo from that day long ago. If she were back home, she'd have gone online to find out the age when permanent memories start to form. There were so many things she took for granted. Science. Knowledge. Freedom.

"So what now?" Amber asked. She folded the flyer on its creases and returned it to her pocket.

"Let's get a good dinner in us. And then I think it's time for a walk-it."

❧

When their row was called, they followed the others toward the back of the room and joined the line that snaked through the schoolroom doors. *Hurry up*, Amber thought as they shuffled forward. *We have places to be and dairy cows to see.* She'd been checking her watch incessantly for the past hour. Time seemed to have sped up again since they'd had their conversation and had jumped another few hours to 3:30 p.m. The change was worrying, but they still had plenty of time. The field trip didn't start until 11:00 a.m. That could still be days away in this world. She felt giddy, or perhaps it was hunger. When they finally made it inside, the aroma of cooked food made Amber's mouth water. She picked up a cafeteria tray and followed the line to a row of serving tables. Women in white PFA shirts doled out fried chicken, green beans, and mashed potatoes.

"We'll need something vegetarian," Sandra told the first helper.

The woman opened a pot and spooned clumped mac 'n' cheese onto their plates.

"Why can't I have chicken?" Amber whined, realizing how immature she sounded, but it felt good to be a petulant tween for a moment.

"Other than the fact that chickens were once living creatures, it's probably equal parts antibiotics, hormones, and hydrogenated vegetable oil. So, no."

Amber, enjoying this brief return to normality, said, "Okay, *Sandra.*"

She took her plate of mac 'n' cheese and green beans. "Thank you," she said to the helper, but the woman just looked past her and said, "Next."

They found a table with open seats. The mothers traded pleasantries as if they were at a community picnic, while reprimanding their children out of the sides of their mouths. "Use a napkin." "Use a fork." "Slow down." "Don't throw green beans on the floor." Every now and then their eyes flickered to the ceiling. But there were no noticeable cameras and everyone seemed relieved to not have to play the egg game.

The mac 'n' cheese on Amber's plate was bright orange, like the box kind that Sandra refused to buy because she said it was mostly chemicals and therefore mislabeled as food. Amber took a bite. She made a face. It did taste artificial, a food impersonator. Just her luck that her taste buds had been ruined by all the years of her mother's unsalted, chemical-free cooking. What she would give right now for one of her mother's pasta dinners.

Sandra must have noticed the pause. "Eat. You'll need it."

A few kids finished eating and wandered to the dessert table, where trays of cookies were set out, protected from eager fingers by a layer of plastic wrap.

Amber shoveled the food into her mouth, barely tasting it, other than an odd tingling on her tongue. Sandra seemed distracted and offered only one reprimand. "Beetle, chew with your mouth closed, please. You're not in an actual farmyard."

After they cleared their plates, Amber and Beetle joined the line of kids waiting for cookies and were each given two. The cookies were the sandwich kind with the filling you could lick. Amber had to admit, if there were cookies at every meal and TV every night, this might not be a bad place to chill while they figured out a plan to get to the dairy farm. But she dreaded the thought of going to "school" here. What would they be taught? How a conveyer belt is proof that the world is flat? How repetitive motion is actually good for the brain?

She wasn't going to find out.

18

When Sandra said "walk-it," Amber had assumed her mother meant around the warehouse floor, but after dinner she told them to gather their things and then steered them down the center aisle, past the rows of cots and through the door they'd entered. Although her mother had said they were free to go, when the door swung closed behind them, Amber expected alarms, crashing gates, and a swarm of guards. Instead, they entered what appeared to be a typical after-hours workplace. Dim hallways. Dark offices. The lingering smell of coffee. The reception desk was unattended.

"This is creepy," Beetle said.

Amber nodded. "I can't believe no one's here."

Sandra tilted her head to the corner, and Amber saw the security camera tracking them as they walked. Obviously, someone was paying attention.

When they pushed on the glass doors, they didn't open. Amber thought, *Aha*, but then Sandra felt around the handle and turned a lock. The door made a sucking sound, as if they'd been inside a space station or a hermetically sealed lab. And it did seem as though they were entering a whole other atmosphere as they left the climate-controlled lobby and waded into air thick with moisture, like a sponge ready to be wrung. It was probably just after dusk, but it was hard to tell with the yellow haze and dark clouds.

Sandra turned to face them. "We're going to have a long walk ahead of us. Just want you to be forewarned."

"You can't mean for us to walk to the dairy farm." Amber seemed to remember that the teacher said it was a thirty-minute drive. And how was Sandra going to find it without a phone or even an old-fashioned map? Amber's backpack pulled on her shoulders. She should have thought to dump the school notebooks in the trash where they belonged.

"We'll head to the apartment and figure it out from there. Maybe someone will stop and offer us a ride. They took my apartment keys, but that front lock is useless, and I left the apartment unlocked."

"We're going to hitchhike? At night?" Amber was incredulous. "And then what?"

Sandra paused. Her brow furrowed and she wrapped her arms around her torso. She studied the ground as if searching for a plan in the muddy tire treads.

Every emotion that Amber had been feeling for the past few days rushed through her like an overflowing river approaching a dam. Why hadn't Sandra thought this through? Did she really not have a better idea than "let's hitchhike home"? *She* was supposed to be the creative one. *She* was the grown-up. None of this would have happened if she'd played by the rules. Not just here, but back home too.

The dam broke. "This is all your fault, Sandra! We never would have ended up in this crazy world if you'd just been normal instead of turning everything into some weird imaginary playland." Amber pointed an accusatory finger. "You said it yourself. We *gave* them an invitation. And now you can't even figure out how to get us home. And you want us to *hitchhike*? Who's going to stop for us other than the police? We should go back inside. At least then we'll be safe."

This idea calmed Amber. That's what common sense dictated. Go back indoors, watch some silly TV shows, sleep on the cots, eat a good breakfast that wasn't burned. At the very least, by waiting until tomorrow, there'd be daylight and maybe the air wouldn't press down so heavily.

Sandra had been silent during Amber's tirade but now she uncurled her arms and stepped forward. "Do you like this world, Amber? Do you?"

Her voice had an edge to it. She kicked loose gravel, which scattered into the puddle by Amber's feet.

Sandra gestured toward the building. "Do you know why worlds like this exist? It's because people are willing to accept that what they're told is normal. They take headlines for granted without digging for nuance. They let technology track their every move, so long as they can play video games on the bus. They wear the clothes they're told to wear. Buy the things they're told they need. Vote for leaders who strip their rights, because they don't have enough imagination to think outside what's being preached to them. Our worlds aren't that far apart, you know. But we don't have to evolve this way." She took a step closer. "The best way we can prevent it is to question the normal, and embrace our uniquely flawed selves with all our wild imaginings."

"But I'm not you," Amber protested. "Maybe all I want is just to fit in for once."

"Oh, Ember," Sandra's voice softened. "You don't get it. I've never wanted you to be like me. All I've ever wanted is for you and Beetle to have the best chance at figuring out how to be *you*. And then for us all to work toward creating a version of a world that accepts you as you are."

They stood in silence while Amber let this sink in. She tapped her toe in the puddle, watched it ripple. She felt the impulse to give her mother a hug, but instead her lips turned up in a part smile, part smirk.

"So, what if the real me isn't a vegetarian?"

"Nice try," Sandra said, returning the smirk. "But some things are still nonnegotiable. At least while you're living at home. Speaking of. It's just a few miles to the apartment. We'll skip the hitchhike and walk. We can rest if you get tired. Ready to try?"

During the argument, Beetle had been studying the parking lot. Now he stuck his arm out of his shirt and pointed toward the side marked *Impound*. "Looks like our car."

Amber followed the direction of Beetle's finger toward a station wagon in a row of similarly well-loved cars.

Sandra took a step, tilted her head. "Sure does."

They walked over and peered through the window. In the light from a nearby lamppost, Amber made out gray curly hairs on the driver's seat headrest, and, in the cup holder, a travel mug that looked like the one her mother owned.

"Maybe the key is in it?" Amber said hopefully.

"No chance," Sandra said. "Remember I couldn't find it when the PFA came?"

Amber tried the door anyway. She circled to try the other doors just in case, and then joined her mother who'd stuck her hands in her pockets and was studying the car, as if she were in a used car lot, considering a purchase.

"I don't believe it," Sandra said. She had a strange look on her face.

"What?" Beetle poked his arms out of his shirt.

Smiling widely, Sandra pulled her hand from her left pocket and unfolded her fingers to reveal a car key in her palm like a pearl in a shell. "Thank you, Witch," she said. "Thank you very, very much."

A white flash lit the sky for a moment, like heat lightning. Amber filed it away with the other occurrences she'd seen as she smiled at her mother. "I bet you had it the entire time."

"Maybe I did, or maybe I didn't," Sandra said as she leaned down to unlock the door. "I once walked around with my credit card in my back pocket for a week before I realized that's where I'd lost it."

Amber climbed into the front seat, while Beetle climbed in back. They both scooched low in their seats. It seemed like the thing to do when making an escape.

"Wooh," Sandra said. "It's one thing to walk out. Far more cinematic to hightail it in stolen property of the state."

She turned the key. The car groaned. She tried again. Another groan.

"You think they'd have known to start it every now and then," Sandra muttered. "Come on, baby, time to get up."

She turned the key, and this time the motor roared like a real baby woken too soon from its nap. Sandra made it worse by squealing backwards out of the parking space and nearly smashed into the car across the row.

"Calm down," she said, as if reprimanding the car for over-eagerness.

The engine sounded louder than normal, as if it were amplified by the thick air (another thing Amber wished she could look up; she should be keeping a list).

Sandra left the headlights off, but before they could get through the main gate, a figure stepped from the shadows. Sandra slammed on the brakes, although they had plenty of distance to stop.

"Is it a guard?" Amber whispered.

"No," Sandra said. She swung open the door but left the car running. "It's Paul."

Amber scooched up far enough to watch her mother approach the man at the gate. He was tall with a trim beard and wore a suit.

Tall. Beard. Paul.

"Beetle," Amber said. She was scared to even hear the words out loud. "I think that's our father."

Sandra and the man spoke for a few minutes. She got back into the car. The man came around the other side. Before he passed, he paused to look through Amber's window. Then Beetle's. His face was in shadow, but Amber thought he looked sad. And nice. He flicked his hand, as if waving them on.

"Mom?" Amber asked, as they turned on the main road. A term unused for so long that it felt funny on her tongue.

"It's okay. He's trying to help. He's just doing it from the inside." Sandra smiled. "He's not so different from your real dad after all. Let's get on the road and I'll tell you more."

When the industrial park was no longer in their sights, Sandra flipped on the headlights and picked up speed.

Amber peered out the rear windshield. "No one's following us."

"Paul may be able to stall them, but there are cameras in the lot. They won't care about us, but taking the car is a crime. They'll assume we're going to the apartment. We'll have to go straight to the dairy farm and find a place to hide out." She smiled wryly. "I was always talking about how I wanted you to have more experience in nature."

Amber hoped her mother wouldn't go off on a tangent about the benefits of the great outdoors. She wanted to hear about Paul. Her father. Dad.

As if Sandra heard Amber's thoughts, she continued. "So, here's the story about your father. He was a labor organizer who got himself into a tough spot after he infiltrated a company to organize their workers. The company caught on and set him up as committing fraud. He was indicted right before Beetle was born. Rather than go to prison, he ran away." She glanced at Amber then looked back at the road. "I didn't tell you because I didn't want you guys to be in a position of having to lie. And I didn't think you were old enough to understand, and then it just didn't seem like the right time. Ever." She shook her head. "We never want to tell our kids things that might hurt them. But of course, keeping secrets can cause a whole different kind of wound."

Amber had so many other questions, but Beetle beat her to the first one when he peeped from the back seat. "Have you heard from him?"

Sandra shook her head. "I think the authorities watched us for a while to see if he would try to make contact. And we had to move a few times at first. It was tough keeping an apartment on hourly wages. It's why you're at Hastings. I wanted you to have some consistency if we had to move again. Truth is, I don't know if the Paul of our world is still alive. But if he is, I'm sure he's doing good somewhere. I miss him."

Amber waited to see if her mother would continue but Sandra seemed lost in her own memories. She wished her mother would tell them a story. A real one this time. About her life before. About Paul. But when her mother stayed silent Amber asked, "Do you really think the witch gave you back the key, or did you just have it and not know?"

Another flash. Was she the only one noticing it? At least, unlike the watch time, the flashes seemed linked to a mention of something (or did the witch count as someone?) from home.

Sandra shrugged. "Usually I'd say it doesn't matter either way. Except now I'd like to believe she's watching out for us, like an old out-of-town friend dropping off a surprise gift. Wouldn't you?"

In the past Amber would have snorted and told Sandra she was being deluded. Or was the word delusional? But her mother was right, there was something comforting about thinking the witch might be close at hand as they headed toward their one, and possibly only, chance to get home.

19

They drove farther west, through places Amber remembered as forest preserve but now contained factories spewing gray smoke into the air. It occurred to Amber that maybe the constantly drab sky wasn't just weather related.

"Do you think the weird color of the sky is from pollution?"

Sandra nodded. "Yup. For all the regulations they've put on families, it sounds like there are almost none on industry. Goodbye, clean air. Hello, smog. Again, don't think it's not happening in our world too. Remember that protest I attended against the new factory by the lake?"

Amber had a vague recollection of Sandra telling them about it. Good to know she could retain information even when her attention drifted. Maybe there was hope in math after all.

"Both of you need to remember that your best defense is to stay informed, stay aware, and stay active." Sandra pounded the steering wheel setting off a bleat of horn, as if the car were saying, "hear, hear." Although the way it huffed down the road suggested it wasn't helping the air quality.

Amber expected her mother to launch into lecture mode, but instead Sandra sighed. "I should have done more to stop that factory. I guess I figured someone with more fight in them would step in and be more active."

Amber thought about how, when her classmates broke the rules, she'd always assumed someone else would take action to stop it. A teacher. Another parent.

"But you *are* active. You get people to vote. Aren't you always telling us that true power is a citizen in a voting booth?"

Sandra smiled. "You always say the right things. You've got a lot of natural leader in you. Just like your father."

Amber blushed, since that contradicted what she'd just been thinking about herself. She turned to face the window so her mother wouldn't see.

They'd left behind the factories and entered a wide expanse of fields, with peeling barns and the occasional huddle of cows. If Amber hadn't been so anxious, she would have found it quite pretty. And reassuring too. Not everything had changed, at least not yet. She could almost believe this was a scene from their own world. Maybe if they drove fast enough, they could plow through some sort of invisible barrier between the two worlds. Or maybe the scene itself could be a touchpoint. An idyllic morning drive.

Now, hold on one real-world second. *Morning* drive?

Amber knew they hadn't been on the road that long, and the clouds made it harder to tell what time it was, but it sure did appear as if the sky was getting lighter. She checked her watch. That couldn't be right. Since the last time she'd looked in the dinner line, the time had changed to 10:40 a.m. She checked the date. SAT APRIL 1. A jump (she rounded to make the mental calculation easier) of nearly fourteen hours! Given the other mother's punctuality, the Parallels could be on the very same road right now!

"Sandra," she waved her watch arm. "The time."

Sandra gave her a confused look, so Amber held her arm steady as Sandra's eyes drifted to the watch, then back to the road.

"Interesting," she said. "I wonder if it's because we're quite literally steering ourselves in our own direction. Bringing the two worlds closer together again. That's pretty wild."

No! Amber wanted to say. *Not wild. Scary. Really scary.* She tried to appear brave, even though her stomach knotted. What if the time at home kept speeding up? Or was time in this world slowing down? Either way, they could miss their chance completely. Once that worry slid in, others stampeded behind.

There were so many reasons this plan wouldn't work—maybe the other Amber hadn't wanted to go, maybe the other mother had to work, maybe Beetle was sick that day, maybe there'd been a big storm, maybe the field trip got canceled, maybe her watch was wrong. She checked again. Could she make it go backwards by pretending to like being here? Or by shouting, "You're stupid!" at the passing cows?

Amber was so focused on her thoughts that it took her a few seconds to notice they'd pulled over. Sandra was rubbing her eyes.

"What are we doing?" Amber asked. "We don't have time to stop."

"We're out of gas."

So much for brave appearances. Amber heard the quake in her voice when she asked, "What are we going to do now?"

Beetle offered the most obvious suggestion. "Walk?"

Sandra unbuckled her seat belt. "I think it's about three miles. You can leave your backpacks unless there's something you need."

Amber rummaged through the bag. Nothing useful unless they could transform notebook sheets into paper airplanes and soar themselves there. Instead she sent a wish, like a silent message in a bottle: *Please help us.* It was simple and vague and not directed toward any specific entity—fairy or otherwise—but it was the only thing she felt she had left as she pushed open the door.

The dirt shoulder was littered with broken bottles, a discarded child seat, and a puddle of something unnaturally green. Far less idyllic than the view from the car window. They kicked up dust as they walked. Long grasses dangling from the shadowed overgrowth seemed on a mission to trip them.

Amber moved closer to the road. Beetle trudged in front

of her, kicking bottles and other garbage out of their path. Amber started to count them. "One. Two. Three."

"Great idea," Sandra said with the enthusiasm she might use to call for a dance-it. "Who's up for singing ninety-nine jars of jam on the wall?"

They'd sung their way down to jar number eighty-two when Amber heard a rumbling. At first she thought it was a storm, the surprising kind that races upon you in summer. But when she turned she spotted a distant light on the road. The knots in her stomach loosened, just a bit.

What if the Parallels really were heading to the farm? And that would create a touchpoint. Then maybe they could wave at themselves in the car windows, and soon the Parallels would be the ones trapped on the roadside in their actual world. She was about tc ask Sandra what she thought of this theory when she noticed that the approaching vehicle had just one orb of light, like a motorcycle. As it rumbled closer it took shape as a larger vehicle with what must have been a broken headlight.

Sandra was already waving her arms. Amber did the same. Beetle extracted an arm from his shirt to join in too. The vehicle stopped, brakes screeching as it kicked up a cloud of dust. It was a van that looked very much like it belonged on the *Impound* parking lot. Through the dust and haze of light, Amber could see swirls of paint on the sides, as if the owner had decided to conceal the van's dents and dings instead of fixing them.

The driver leaned over and unrolled the passenger window. He was an older man with flowing white hair. "You broken down?"

"Yes," Sandra said. "But we don't have far to go. Just to Carlton's Dairy Farm."

"Happy to get you there," he said.

Sandra climbed into the passenger seat, and Amber and Beetle scrambled over her legs and through the two front seats to get into the back. There were wood shavings on the van floor, and something that looked like a tool chest, and whittled wood pieces that could perhaps be legs for a table. The van possessed the comforting smell of cedar, reminding Amber of the hamster cage from her second-grade classroom.

"I'm a woodworker," the man offered. "Name's Charlie."

"Sandra."

Amber thought her mother should have used an alias. Perhaps this was a setup and he was really a PFA agent in disguise who would whisk them back to the warehouse. Or to one of the factories, where kids were forced to do hard labor, and instead of cookies, brussels sprouts were served every day.

There were no seats in the back so Amber and Beetle sat on the floor next to the tool chest. The ride was bumpy but no worse than riding in the back row of a school bus. Although Charlie did seem to drive faster than your average bus driver. Quite fast, in fact. From where she sat, Amber could see her mother grasp the door handle. Amber almost liked the feeling of being rattled around, since it suited the jumbled condition of her mind.

"Amber." Beetle's voice jiggled with the movement. "I think it's Mr. Zagoom."

"What?"

"Mr. Zagoom."

"Beetle, there's no need for your secret word. It's me, okay?"

But now that Beetle said it, the connection slid into her imagination like a puzzle piece. Spray-painted van, check. White-haired wizard-y driver, check. Cautious driver. Most certainly not. Every few minutes the van swerved, and Amber and Beetle had to grab each other to keep from pitching to the other side. Then again, he could just be a parallel Mr. Zagoom, or whatever the man's actual name was. Just to cover all bases, Amber pretended Beetle was right, and Sandra's story was true, and Mr. Zagoom was some sort of magical world jumper. None of this mattered unless he could turn at the next intersection and whisk them home. Otherwise, the only thing that did matter was to stay focused on their goal: get to Carlton's Dairy Farm.

Amber checked her watch. It was too hard to read in the darkened van and with her arm jiggling. She wasn't sure how long the field trip would last. She pictured Debbie and Clara with their impeccable mothers, maybe their fathers too, along with the Parallels, who were probably doing a way better job at fitting in than she and Beetle had done in this world, or their own. Then she thought about what her mother had said in the parking lot. About the risk of trying so hard to be normal. It made her think of Darwin and his theory of natural selection. If more people accepted things as they were, would that be the trait that spread? If so, then her mother was right, and their world was already a lot closer to this one than Amber would like to believe.

The van skidded to a stop. Amber crashed into Beetle, who crashed into the back of Charlie's seat.

"Thank you," Sandra said. She sounded breathless, and Amber couldn't tell if she was thanking him for giving them a lift or because this roller coaster of a ride had ended.

Amber scrambled out after Beetle. They'd pulled up next to a wooden sign with Carlton's Dairy Farm painted on it and an arrow pointing up an unlit dirt road. A padlock dangled off a metal gate, barring entry. Next to it was a narrow footpath.

"Sure this is where you want to go?"

"Yes, thank you," Sandra said. "We'll walk up. We know someone here."

Amber was not used to hearing her mother lie. Even with all the stories Sandra told, Amber considered her to be an honest person. At least she wasn't just blabbing their story to a total stranger. But they had to hurry. What if the tour was over?

"That path looks pretty dark. Might help to have one of these." Charlie handed Sandra a flashlight. When she tried to decline, he smiled. "You can return it later." He handed her a business card. "Number's on here. In case you're ever looking for custom woodworking, and I'm handy at fixing other things too."

Sandra thanked him, tucked the card in her pocket, and grasped the flashlight.

The van sped away. Amber closed her eyes and waited for the road dust to settle. She needed a minute on solid ground for her legs to steady. She assumed the others did too. When she opened her eyes she saw her mother watching her.

Sandra smiled. "All for one and one for ice cream. Take a deep breath. We're getting close."

Amber did as suggested. She smelled cows and grass and mud, and a faint hint of something that she couldn't name but made her think, *Home*!

Sandra turned on the flashlight. Amber wanted to run up the footpath to reach the other side, but she followed the slower pace of the flashlight beam. At one point a shadow with two bright eyes crossed the path. Beetle squeaked in alarm, and Sandra dropped the flashlight. When she picked it up, the eyes were gone.

The path ended as the road widened to the entry point of the farm. Light posts bathed the area in a pool of soft light although the sky was light enough to see. Amber spotted a building with a large *Welcome Center* sign next to a large barn. Gentle mooing came from the barn's vicinity. Off this main area, three smaller roads jutted in different directions. A large bird flew overhead and settled in a tree. Did they have owls here? Amber had always wanted to see a real owl.

"Where do you think we should go?" Sandra asked.

Amber felt as if she was being asked to solve a math

problem on a topic that hadn't been covered in class. How do you calculate the distance between two objects moving at different speeds *and* in different spheres of time? And then, to make it even more challenging, also make the time difference arbitrary. She wished the fairy godmother would come back with a suggestion. But when no voice appeared, she took another deep breath and opened her mind.

The first thing that flew in was the trash-can rule. Yes, of course. If they started walking around the dairy farm, and the Parallels were also walking around, they might never run into each other.

"We should pick one spot to wait," she said. Her mind extended it into a silent rhyme: *and hope we're not too late.*

Sandra nodded. "How about the last place on the tour. Maybe the parking lot? We could look for the car or check puddles."

Beetle pointed to a sign that read *Gift Shop.*

"Good thinking, Beetle," Sandra said.

They followed the path to what might at one time have been a storage shack. It had a red door and a large display window with *Carlton's Gifts* painted on it in old-fashioned loopy letters and the faces of smiling cows on either side. Amber tried to peer in. The store was dark. The window reflected their images. Amber's breath quickened. Was this it? She waved. The Amber in the window waved. She smiled. The image smiled. Sandra and Beetle mimicked her moves and the images in the window did the same, as if they were performing an amateur dance routine.

"Now what?" Amber asked.

She heard the catch in her voice and tried to block the running list of the many reasons their plan might fail: it wasn't Magic Hour, the Parallels didn't want to switch, they might have already missed their window. The last one made her giggle out of nervousness.

"What's funny?" Beetle asked.

She told him. "Get it? We lost our window of opportunity, which is literally a window."

Beetle joined in Amber's giggle.

Their mother smiled. "That's very reflective of you."

"Doesn't look like we're missing our window. Looks like it's right here." Amber tapped on the glass.

Then the three of them were chortling. It wasn't that funny a joke, or maybe even funny at all, but laughter will do that sometimes, well up and overflow. It felt like air escaping an overfilled balloon, or a rainstorm streaming the dirt off their never-washed car.

Sandra held her hand to her stomach. "Can't...catch... my...breath."

Amber wiped tears from her eyes, and that's when she noticed the change.

"Sandra." She grabbed her mother by the arm, the laughter gone as suddenly as it came on. "They're watching us!"

20

It was true. In the window, the three reflected figures no longer matched the movements of Amber, Beetle, and Sandra. Instead they stood stiffly, with looks of surprise and perhaps even fear. The mother in the window had very short hair.

Sandra grabbed Amber and Beetle by the hands and pulled them forward, marching them directly into the glass.

Amber shut her eyes. She expected to hear shattering, or feel glass shards slice her face, but instead she felt a different kind of resistance, as if fighting her way upstream against frigid whitewater rapids. She couldn't catch her breath and worried her hand would be wrenched from her mother's. She tightened her grip and felt herself get pulled forward a step. And then another. The air stilled. She opened her eyes.

They stood in front of the gift shop, facing the window, as if they hadn't moved at all. But other things had changed—most noticeably the light. It was as if the sun were shining directly on top of them, so bright that it washed out their surroundings. There were new sounds, too—raucous mooing, laughter, and music. Actual music. Some type of country tune with a fiddle. No wait, it was something familiar. "Old McDonald had a Farm." Amber realized that was something else she'd been missing. When was the last time they'd heard music outdoors?

She blinked a few times as her eyes struggled to adjust. She saw Beetle and her mother reflected in the window. But no. These reflections stretched to the ground and were three-dimensional. They weren't reflections. They were the Parallels. The Parallels who were standing in front of the window, not inside of it.

One thing that did match was the look of astonishment on all their faces.

"How—?" Amber asked, unable to finish her sentence.

Sandra—the Sandra standing next to Amber—gripped her hand tighter, as if worried Amber might blow away, although there was only a gentle breeze.

"Hello, Sandra," Amber's mother said.

"Hello," the other mother replied. "I go by Sandy." Her lips flickered in a tight smile. She also gripped the hands of her children and leaned away, as if preparing to jump back through the window.

Amber stared at her parallel self. The other version was wearing the heart shirt. Amber wondered where she'd found it, or if perhaps finding it in one world had allowed it to turn up in the other. The other girl no longer had the haughty expression from before. She dropped her mother's hand and looked down.

"I thought you said we couldn't be in the same world together," Amber said and pulled her own hand free, as if following a compulsion to mirror her parallel self. And which world was it? Were they still in the Parallels'? The sunlight suggested otherwise. Then that meant they were back in their own world. Either way it was clear something had gone wrong because they shouldn't all be standing together. "Where are we?" Amber demanded, with a slight quiver in her voice.

Sandra tilted her head. "Interesting."

"What?" Amber demanded.

"I think, and correct me if I'm wrong," she said to the other mother, "That we're somewhere in between."

Sandy nodded, her bobbed hair dancing on her shoulders. "Perhaps someplace entirely new."

"I don't understand," Parallel Beetle said. He scuffed the dirt with the toe of his shoe. He looked scared.

Amber wanted to reach over and give him a reassuring

punch, but, of course, he wasn't her actual brother. He was the one who had stolen her brother's place and tricked her into crossing too.

But Amber wasn't feeling angry now. Or even as scared as before. Safety in numbers and all that. This would surely stump the PFA.

"Let's go sit for a moment," Sandra said. Her eyes flickered to the window. As Amber followed she glanced at it too. Even though they were passing in front of it, the window was empty of their images. Like losing your shadow. Or becoming invisible. A trick of the light, Amber assumed. Yet another thing to look up.

They walked to a shaded spot under an oak tree and sat in a circle. Amber crossed her legs, this time feeling like she was back in kindergarten with so much left to learn. It felt good to sit. She leaned back on her hands. Around them families headed up and down the paths while younger kids raced ahead. A few clusters followed that must be school groups. No one paid attention to them or even seemed to notice that there were three sets of identical twins. Maybe they really were invisible?

"Let's review what we understand about parallel universes," Sandra began, as if she were one of the educational tour guides. "Let's say, for the sake of argument, every possible outcome exists in a world somewhere. If so, I was wrong because that would mean there *was* a world where we could all exist together in the same space. But what I don't understand is why we wouldn't have just swapped back into our rightful universes? Us back to ours, you to yours?"

"I didn't want to go back," the other Amber blurted out, her voice rising. "You said we'd never have to go back."

A look from her mother lowered her volume but not her intensity. "I want to play sports and walk places on my own. What about my new friends?" She glanced at Amber. "Sorry, but Clara and Debbie might not want to hang out with you."

"They didn't want to before. Good riddance," Amber said.

The other Beetle looked up. "I wished that too. I like that you can ask questions in school and play any game you want, anytime you want, and that it isn't weird to not have a dad."

Beetle popped an arm out of his shirt and gave a thumbs-up.

Amber wondered again how much they knew about their father. She experienced a flash of superiority, and the tug of a haughty twitch to her lips. That must be the influence of the world they'd just left, stuck to her like the dust of travel. She swiped her hand over her face, as if to brush it away.

"I wished the same," Sandy said. She stretched out her legs and ran her fingers through her hair, as if to confirm it was still the appropriate length. "I just wished for any place better, although maybe one with more income potential. I can't imagine how you were able to make ends meet. Was there any improvement after you arrived?"

Sandra shook her head. "Worse." She filled the Parallels in on what had been happening, the roundups and the factories, the growing list of ridiculous rules and restrictions.

Amber picked at the grass. The *green* grass. There was a different feeling where they were now—a different *vibe*—as if the air currents had changed from whitewater rapids to the gentle flow of a stream. She wondered if the other Amber was feeling it too. She looked over and smiled. The other girl smiled back. She had also been picking at the grass, but her nails were painted purple. Amber never painted her nails (one game of catch would destroy them) but if she had to paint them, she'd probably pick purple polish. It was like having a clone, but not. She was beginning to feel less than herself, as if she were losing her own sense of "Amberness." She spotted a crumpled newspaper nearby. She stretched to pick it up, then tossed it between her hands like a ball. That was better.

Sandy snorted.

"If only the others knew that it didn't have to be that way."

Amber assumed Sandy was referring to all the mothers still trapped in that gray, dark place. And her sort-of father. They'd left him behind too, and she'd never even gotten a chance to talk to him. A lump formed in her throat. She wondered if Beetle had been thinking about him too?

She looked at the two Beetles seated next to each other, but the light was still too bright for her to tell which one wore the blue stretched-out shirt. What if, when it was time to go, they paired off wrong?

"The witch," she announced.

The Beetle on the right replied, "Mr. Zagoom."

This time, no flash of light. But maybe it was too bright to notice.

"I still don't get it," the other Amber said. "Why weren't we sent back to our world?"

"I think it's because you're not the same person," Sandra told her. "When your awareness changed, and your attitudes and desires, you created a new world. Same with us." She put her hand on Amber's leg, as if she, too, needed reminding of who belonged to whom. "Every time we brought in a thought or a memory that wasn't from that world, we generated another option. And I think, today, those world versions moved us back toward each other."

"Every action causes an equal and opposite reaction," Beetle said.

"Show-off," Amber said. She tossed the ball up and leaned over to catch it when the breeze changed its course. She didn't have anything to offer the conversation except confusion. She wondered if the creation of this new world had anything to do with the flashes of light. If so, had that been happening in her world too? She would need some time to let it all settle in. Ha, time. She didn't know if she had more of it or less of it. She looked at her watch, but it didn't mean anything. The touchpoint idea had failed. What would they do if they all got stuck here? Share the same apartment? Would she and the other Amber trade school days? Amber remembered the other girl's academic background and sighed. Maybe she could be the one to go on test days.

"Is this a good place?" the other Beetle asked.

Amber's instinct suggested it was. The air smelled sweet. The sun shone brighter. There was music, and laughter, and those softer currents of air. For the first time since she'd discovered the other mother, she felt almost safe. Although it would be helpful to know where and when they were. For all she knew it was the middle of winter but climate change had taken over. She wished she could stop one of the tour guides and ask, "Excuse me, can you tell me what month and year this is?"

Really, Amber? The fairy godmother was back. *The answer is in your hands.*

Great, another snarky hint. Amber tossed the ball up and caught it. Oh, wait. She uncrumpled the paper. It was the front page of the *News Herald*. She checked the date: just one week after they'd left their own world. The top headline read *Governor Belling pledges support for Paid Family Leave*. Amber scanned the article.

"Look at this!"

She handed the paper to her mother, who read aloud, "After narrowly defeating incumbent Ron G. Vernon last fall, Belling has continued to make strides on her promise to improve the lives of all constituents." Sandra looked up and smiled. "Her." She read on about Belling's accomplishments, but her smile dimmed when she got to the part about the growing efforts of a coalition of state representatives who advocated for more regulatory action to protect and preserve traditional families.

It wasn't perfect here, but it was better.

The mothers stood and rubbed their knees.

Sandra extended a hand. "It's very nice to finally meet you."

Sandra and Sandy shook hands. Amber had a flash of worry that touching would jar yet another strange shift in the world, and the two women would suddenly merge into one.

"It's very nice to finally meet you too," Sandy said. "And I'm sorry. I really am. To put you through that. I just couldn't think of any other way."

"I understand," Sandra said. "And it was for the best. It made this other world possible."

For a few moments no one spoke, just traded shy glances at one another. Amber felt as if she were at a middle school dance.

"So what now?" Amber asked.

While they'd been seated, the sun had passed overhead and was sinking in the other direction, leaving a trail of pink tendrils.

"Almost Magic Hour," Amber's mother said. She turned to Sandy. "The car's about three miles east. Sorry, it's out of gas."

Sandy said, "You should know a crazy van driver knocked the side mirror off your car. I'd been meaning to get it fixed."

"That reminds me." Sandra took the business card out of her pocket, glanced at it, and passed it to Sandy with the flashlight. "If you get a chance, can you return this? You might find him handy."

Sandy placed the card and flashlight in her purse. She took the hands of her Amber and Beetle. Neither pulled away. "Let's see if we can't find ourselves a ride."

They started down the path with the arrow marked *Office*.

Sandra led Amber and Beetle the opposite way to the gift shop. She stopped in front of the window.

"What are we doing?" Amber asked. The thought of being trapped here wasn't nearly as frightening as before. It might even be fun to have a twin. A true doppelgänger. Oh, the pranks they could play. But it would be good to be home. Their real home. If she was going to be an outsider, she'd much rather be one inside her own universe.

"They left the door ajar. Look."

The window's glass had a watery shimmer. In the reflection Amber saw the barn and the tree they'd been sitting under and the driveway to the main road. But, just as before, their images were missing.

"I think we're being invited home," Sandra said.

She grasped their hands, and they stepped forward without resistance, crossing through the windowsill as if boarding a waiting train.

Epilogue: Home

21

Amber's alarm jangled. She opened her eyes and saw the clean floor of her bedroom. A pile of clothes folded on her desk. Had she dreamed their escape? But then her recent memory woke up too. She remembered how they'd returned to find an impeccable apartment. Even the closets! Sandy was a neat freak for sure.

Amber checked her watch. Seven a.m.

She looked at the alarm clock. It matched!

She sat up and looked at her bulletin board, marveling at the disarray. She took a gulp of air. Smelled its mix of smells that could never be identified individually but added up to the mishmash of scents that combined into "home." There was a new smell too, something that smelled a lot like scrambled eggs. Perhaps some good had come out of this strange, terrible adventure after all.

In the kitchen, she found Beetle at the table, scarfing down breakfast. Sandra was seated across from him with a cup of coffee. Amber's eyes drifted to the corner of the ceiling. No egg camera. She wanted to cheer. The sunlight streamed through the window, strong and bright. But not so bright that it hurt her eyes. Just the right amount of bright. Everything felt just right.

"Sandy left us completely reorganized," Sandra said. "I can't find a darn thing." The way she smiled made it clear she didn't care. Her hair circled her head in a disheveled, wild mess. "We timed the return well—it's Sunday. Will you be okay on your own today?"

Amber helped herself to a scoop of eggs and reached for the juice. "Of course. We're not *babies*. Where are you going?"

"To a volunteer meeting at the office of our congressional representative. Time for me to get back in the game. There's a lot at stake." She reached over and tucked a strand of Amber's hair behind her ear. "Tonight, let's have a family meeting. I made a mistake by not sharing more about Paul with you. He was a hero. And in that other world, I know he'll continue to be one."

Amber nodded, although she felt her throat tighten. Beetle gave a thumbs-up.

"Well, Little Bug," Amber said through a mouthful of eggs. "I say we go to the park." She rotated her arm and stretched it over her head. It was stiff. Too stiff.

Beetle brought his plate to the sink (another lesson learned!) and left to fetch his soccer ball. Amber stayed at the table. She didn't want to think about what she might face on Monday at school—what had happened to her grades? Who were her new friends? But she also found she didn't really care as she listened to a car drive by with music blaring and the birds chirp in the trees. The air felt electric, as if charged with Amber's anticipation of all that was possible.

She watched as her mother sipped coffee, a faraway smile, crazy hair streaming, her blouse already splotched. Amber felt like she needed to say something but wasn't sure what. Thank you for saving us? For doing what you do every single day to take care of us? How could she possibly say everything she was thinking and feeling?

As Sandra carried her mug to the sink, Amber looked out the window at the world—*her* world—in all its beauty and freedom, and whispered, "I'm glad you're my mom."

"What's that, sweetie?"

Amber stood too. "I said I'll do the dishes. Also, it's okay if we have pasta tonight."

Sandra smiled. "Oh, don't worry, we will be." She stood by the kitchen counter. "Now if I were Sandy, where would I have put my house keys? Witch, could use some help here."

Amber carried her plate and glass to the sink.

"That's something I don't understand," Amber said as she soaped a sponge. "About all the made-up stuff. I mean how did we get those lunch notes and did the witch really help us? Or the fairy godmother in my head? I mean, was any of it real?"

Sandra paused her search. "I like to believe we create the world we want to live in. When we needed the witch and the others, we called on them. Maybe it was the witch who gave you those notes. Or a fairy. Or they were delivered by yet another version of me. The only *real* thing we can be sure about when it comes to reality is that it contains the letters *R*,*E*,*A*, and *L*."

"But how do we *know* anything?" Amber asked as she scrubbed the plate. "Beetle even had this crazy idea that that van driver was Mr. Zagoom."

Amber checked her mother's reaction. Sandra had never told them what was on the business card she'd given to Sandy. But she was busy digging through a drawer in search of the keys.

"I think it's okay to not know one way or the other. I think some truths prefer to reside in our imaginations, and we should let them. Can you believe she alphabetized my coupons?"

"C'mon, Amber," Beetle called from the door.

"Go ahead," Sandra said. "The dishes can wait."

Amber ran to fetch her mitt. How good it felt to stick her hand into something that fit so well. Her fingers wiggled a hello. Time to show the boys at the park how to throw someone out from first. Who knew, maybe the game would get her into college someday. Or maybe all it would do was bring her joy. Either way, it was time to play ball.

Acknowledgments

With gratitude to all the teachers, mentors and friends who helped guide this book's journey. Special thanks to Jaynie Royal, Elizabeth Lowenstein, and the team at Fitzroy Books; I'm so proud to be part of your thriving community of writers. Also to Amanda Friedman who gave early feedback (and reassurance) when I most needed it; Fred Shafer and Jan English Leary for over a decade of encouragement and literary wisdom; Suzanne Barefoot, for her sharp eye, generous heart, and willingness to answer emails that began "morning meltdown"; my parents, for their weekly trips to the library and knowing that an electric typewriter would make a good gift for a young bookworm; and to my husband and children for being the best cheering squad any fledgling writer could hope to have.